WHISKEY, WANDERLUST, AND WOVEN TALES

JORDAN POOLE

FOREWORD

~

Dear wanderer of words and connoisseur of cocktails,

You're about to embark on a journey through time, place, and spirits. Each tale in this collection is a carefully crafted cocktail of narrative, best enjoyed in three distinct acts. Here's how to savor each story to its fullest:

Act 1: The Spirits

Begin by mixing the featured cocktail. As you prepare your drink, let the aromas and flavors transport you to the setting of our story. This is your invitation to the story—your ticket to a new world.

Act 2: The Tale

Sip slowly as you read the main story. Let the flavors of your drink mingle with the unfolding narrative. Each sip should be a punctuation mark in the tale, a moment to pause and reflect on the characters and their journey.

Act 3: The Ponderance

As your glass nears empty and the story concludes, take time to contemplate. This final act is for reflection, where the aftertaste of your drink mingles with the lingering thoughts provoked by the tale.

Remember, like any good cocktail, these stories are meant to be savored. Take your time, let the flavors develop, and don't hesitate to mix another as you lose yourself in the narrative.

Cheers to your journey, fellow gypsy! May your glass and imagination always be full.

INTRODUCTION

The Spirit of Wanderlust

In an age where the world seems to shrink with each passing day, where technology connects us across vast distances and cultural boundaries blur like watercolors on a rain-soaked canvas, there exists a curious paradox: the more connected we become, the more we yearn for authentic experiences, for tastes and sensations that can't be captured in a tweet or an Instagram story. It's in this intersection of global connectivity and the search for the genuinely local that the concept of the "Postmodern Gypsy" is born.

But what exactly is a postmodern gypsy? It's a state of mind, a way of moving through the world with open eyes and an open heart, collecting stories and flavors like precious stones, each one unique and irreplaceable. The Postmodern Gypsy is a traveler, yes, but one who seeks not just to see new places but to immerse themselves in the very essence of each locale they visit.

As a Postmodern Gypsy, I've learned that the joy of travel isn't just in the destinations we reach, but in the journey itself. It's in the unexpected detours, the chance encounters, the moments of serendipity that no guidebook can predict. And often, these moments happen around a bar, over a drink, in the company of strangers who quickly become friends.

Pack your bags, loosen your tie, and prepare your palate. The journey of the postmodern gypsy is about to begin, and the first round is on me. Let's toast to the journey ahead and all the tales we have yet to share, one drink at a time.

1

SPIRITS OF CHANGE

Act 1. The Spirits: Jack and Coke

In the heart of Savannah, where Spanish moss drapes over centuries-old oaks and whispers of the past mingle with dreams of the future, a simple cocktail became the unlikely catalyst for transformation. This is not just a recipe for a Jack and Coke; it's a toast to new beginnings, to finding clarity in the most unexpected places, and to the courage it takes to chase a vision—even if that vision arrives at the bottom of a whiskey glass.

As the day winds down and the evening stretches before you, a craving for something familiar yet satisfying takes hold. Your mind settles on a classic: the Jack and Coke.

You begin by selecting a sturdy rock glass from your shelf. Its weight in your hand feels reassuring, a promise of good things to come. With a practiced motion, you fill the glass with ice cubes, their crystalline surfaces catching the soft light of your kitchen.

Next comes the star of the show - the bottle of Jack Daniel's Old No. 7. You lift it with reverence, feeling the weight of tradition in your hands. As you pour a generous double shot over the ice, the amber liquid cascades down, weaving through the cracks between the cubes. The rich aroma of Tennessee whiskey fills the air, hinting at oak, vanilla, and a touch of sweetness.

Now for the counterpart to Jack's bold character - the Coca-Cola. You reach for a cold can or bottle, its surface beaded with condensation. With a satisfying crack or hiss, you open it, releasing that unmistakable scent of caramel and spice. Slowly, you pour the cola over the whiskey and ice, watching as it froths and bubbles, creating a perfect amber-brown blend.

The ratio is key here; you aim for one part Jack to three parts Coke, adjusting slightly to suit your taste. As the drink comes together, you observe how the colors meld, creating a rich, inviting hue that seems to glow from within the glass.

For a finishing touch, you decide to add a slice of lime. You cut a wedge from a fresh lime, its citrusy scent providing a bright counterpoint to the sweet and smoky aromas already present. You run the lime around the rim of the glass before dropping it gently into the drink, adding a subtle twist to the classic combination.

You step back and admire your creation. Jack and Coke stands before you, deceptively simple yet undeniably appealing. Condensation beads form on the outside of the glass, promising a cool, refreshing experience.

As you lift the drink to your lips, the mingled aromas of whiskey, cola, and a hint of lime greet you. The first sip is a perfect balance - the smooth, oaky warmth of Jack Daniel's harmonizing with the sweet, effervescent Coke. The lime adds just a touch of brightness, elevating the entire experience.

In this moment, you realize that you've created more

than just a drink. This Jack and Coke is a testament to the beauty of simplicity, a reminder that sometimes the most satisfying things in life are the ones we know by heart. As you settle into your favorite chair, drink in hand, you can't help but appreciate how this unpretentious cocktail can turn an ordinary evening into something special. This, you think, is the perfect way to unwind and savor the simple pleasures of life. As you sip your perfectly mixed Jack and Coke, let its familiar warmth remind you of the power of embracing the unexpected. You might find that the path to your dreams isn't always straight or conventional. Sometimes a detour through a hardware store or a late-night conversation fueled by liquid courage is required.

I've got a weakness for hardware stores and the characters you find in 'em. Well, this story comes from one of the most fabulous ladies I've ever met behind a counter full of nuts and bolts. She shared with me a tale of an unexpected date she once had—with a bottle of Jack Daniels.

But don't let that fool you. This isn't just another drunk story. No, my friends, this is a modern retelling of an age-old truth. The Romans had a saying: "In vino veritas" - in wine, there is truth. Well, it seems in whiskey, there might just be visions.

Act 2. The Tale: A Date with Jack Daniels

The bell above the door chimed as Curt and Eleanor entered Joni's Hardware, blissfully unaware that a bottle of Jack Daniels was about to change their lives forever. The familiar scent of sawdust and metal greeted them, along with the booming voice of Joni herself.

"Well, if it ain't my favorite DIY disaster couple!" Joni called out from behind the counter, her purple-streaked blonde hair catching the light as she turned. "What're we fixin' today?"

Curt, with his neatly trimmed beard and thick-rimmed glasses, sheepishly held up a broken doorknob. "Hey Joni, we had a bit of an incident with the upstairs bathroom door."

Eleanor, balancing their two-year-old daughter Pearl on her hip, rolled her eyes. "He means he tried to be macho and kicked it open when it got stuck."

Joni let out a hearty laugh that seemed to shake the shelves. "Lord, honey, you're lucky you didn't put your foot through that old wood! Come on back, I'll show you what you need."

As they followed Joni through the narrow aisles, Eleanor couldn't help but marvel at the organized chaos of the store. Every nook and cranny was filled with tools, hardware, and odds and ends that she couldn't even name. It was a far cry from the sleek non-profit office she'd worked in until a few weeks ago.

"So, Eleanor," Joni said, rifling through a bin of doorknobs, "how's the job hunt going? Any leads?"

Eleanor sighed, bouncing Pearl gently as the toddler started to fuss. "Not really. It's been tough out there, especially with my background in non-profit work. I'm starting to wonder if I should look into something completely different."

Joni paused, a thoughtful look crossing her face. "You know, that reminds me of how I ended up openin' this place. It's quite a story – you got time for a little tale?"

Curt and Eleanor exchanged glances. They'd learned early on that Joni's "little tales" were rarely short, but always entertaining.

"Sure," Curt said, leaning against a shelf. "We've got nowhere else to be."

Joni's eyes lit up. "Well, pull up a paint can and get comfy. This is the story of how Jack Daniels helped me find my true callin'."

Eleanor raised an eyebrow, but Pearl settled on her lap as they sat on overturned buckets.

"Now, this was about fifteen years ago," Joni began, her voice taking on a storyteller's cadence. "I was workin' at Gulfstream, doin' supply chain management. I thought I had it made – good salary, benefits, the whole nine yards. Then one day, out of nowhere, they called us all into a big meeting. Downsizing, they said. Restructuring. All those fancy words that really just mean 'You're fired.'"

Eleanor winced, the memory of her own recent layoff still fresh.

"I was devastated," Joni continued. "Didn't know what I was gonna do. I mean, I had my mama to take care of and bills to pay. That night, I went home and decided I was going to have myself a pity party. Just me and a bottle of Jack Daniels."

Curt chuckled. "Sounds like a recipe for disaster."

"Oh, honey, you have no idea," Joni said with a wink. "I started drinkin' straight from the bottle, cryin' and cussin' and carryin' on something fierce. Poor Mama thought I'd lost my mind. By midnight, I was three sheets to the wind and practically howlin' at the moon."

Eleanor found herself leaning in, captivated by Joni's animated storytelling.

"Now, here's where it gets interesting," Joni said, lowering her voice conspiratorially. "Somewhere around two in the morning, in my Jack Daniels-induced haze, I had what I can only describe as a vision. I saw myself standin' behind this very counter, helpin' folks like you two figure out how to fix up their homes. It was so clear, so vivid – I could practically smell the sawdust."

"But why a hardware store?" Curt asked, genuinely curious.

Joni shrugged. "Hell if I know. Maybe it was because my dad used to drag me to the hardware store every weekend when I was a kid. Or maybe it was just the universe's way of givin' me a kick in the pants. All I know is, when I woke up the next morning with a headache that could kill a horse, that vision was still there, clear as day."

Eleanor found herself nodding, a spark of recognition igniting in her chest. She'd been feeling so lost since losing her job, but listening to Joni's story, she felt a glimmer of... something. Hope? Inspiration?

"Of course," Joni continued, "openin' a business ain't exactly a walk in the park. I had to cash in my 401k, take out loans, and learn more about nuts and bolts than I ever thought possible. Mama thought I'd gone off the deep end for sure. But you know what? Every step of the way, even when things got tough, I never doubted that this was what I was meant to do."

"And now look at you," Curt said, gesturing around the packed store. "Savannah's hardware queen."

Joni let out another booming laugh. "I don't know about queen, but I do alright. More importantly, I wake up every day lovin' what I do. Can't put a price on that."

As Joni finished her story, Eleanor felt a strange mix of emotions swirling in her chest. Part of her wanted to laugh at the absurdity of finding one's life purpose at the bottom of a whiskey bottle. But another part – a growing part – felt a sense of longing. When was the last time she'd felt that kind of clarity about her path?

"Anyway," Joni said, snapping back to the present, "that's enough of my yammerin'. Let's get you fixed up with that doorknob before Pearl here decides to redecorate my store."

As they made their way to the register, Eleanor's mind was buzzing. She barely registered Curt paying for the doorknob and thanking Joni. It wasn't until they were back out on Tattnall Street, the humid Savannah air enveloping them, that Curt's voice broke through her reverie.

"You okay, hon? You seem a million miles away."

Eleanor blinked, adjusting Pearl on her hip. "Yeah, I'm fine. Just... thinking."

Curt gave her a knowing look. "About Joni's story?"

She nodded. "It's crazy, right? But also... I don't know. Kind of inspiring?"

As they walked back to their Victorian fixer-upper, Eleanor's mind raced. She thought about her years working for the non-profit, the sense of purpose she'd felt. But if she was honest with herself, that feeling had faded long before the layoff. She'd been going through the motions, telling herself it was meaningful work, but the passion had dimmed.

That night, after they'd put Pearl to bed and Curt had successfully installed the new doorknob (with only minor swearing), Eleanor found herself standing in front of the liquor cabinet. She pulled out a bottle of Jack Daniels they'd received as a housewarming gift, studying it thoughtfully.

"El?" Curt's voice startled her. He was leaning against the doorframe, a puzzled expression on his face. "You're not actually considering Joni's method, are you?"

Eleanor laughed, but it sounded hollow even to her own ears. "I don't know. Maybe? I just... I feel so lost, Curt. Like I'm drifting without a purpose. And hearing Joni talk about finding her calling, even if it was through unconventional means... it made me realize how much I want that feeling."

Curt crossed the room, wrapping his arms around her from behind. "I get it. But maybe we can find a slightly less liver-damaging way to figure things out?"

Eleanor leaned back into him, grateful for his solid presence. "You're probably right. It's just... when did we become so responsible? So... safe?"

Curt chuckled, his breath warming against her ear. "Probably around the time we had Pearl and decided to buy a falling-down Victorian and turn it into an Airbnb."

She turned into his arms, a mischievous glint in her eye. "You know what? Let's do it. Let's have our own Jack Daniels vision quest."

Curt's eyebrows shot up. "Are you serious?"

"Dead serious," Eleanor said, already reaching for glasses. "We'll make a pact. Tonight, we drink and we talk – really talk – about what we want. No holding back, no practical considerations. Just raw, drunken honesty. And tomorrow..."

"We nurse our hangovers and hope we remember our revelations?" Curt finished with a grin spreading across his face.

"Exactly."

An hour later, they were sprawled on the old hardwood floor of what would eventually be their Airbnb's living room. The Jack Daniels bottle was significantly emptier, and their inhibitions had lowered considerably.

"Okay," Eleanor slurred slightly, propping herself up on an elbow. "If you could do anything – and I mean anything – what would it be?"

Curt took a long swig straight from the bottle. "Honestly? I'd quit law and open a bakery."

Eleanor burst out laughing. "A bakery? You can barely make toast!"

"Hey, I said anything!" Curt protested, but he was laughing too. "I've always loved the idea of it. The smell of fresh bread makes people happy with food. Plus, no more billable hours or stuffy partners breathing down my neck."

As their laughter subsided, Eleanor felt a warmth that wasn't just from the whiskey. She loved seeing this side of Curt – the dreamer beneath the responsible lawyer exterior.

"Your turn," Curt said, poking her gently. "What's Eleanor's wild dream?"

She closed her eyes, letting the question really sink in. What did she want when all the practicalities and expectations were stripped away?

"I want to start a community art center," she said finally, the words tumbling out. "A place where kids and adults can come to create, to express themselves. With classes and exhibitions and... I don't know, maybe even a little cafe."

As soon as she said it, Eleanor felt a surge of excitement. It was as if she'd uncovered a long-buried desire she didn't even know she had.

Curt sat up, his eyes bright despite the alcohol. "El, that's brilliant! It combines your non-profit background with your art degree. And God knows Savannah could use more community spaces like that."

They spent the next few hours drunkenly planning their new ventures – debating cupcake flavors and art class schedules, giggling over potential names and logos. As the night wore on and the bottle emptied, their plans grew increasingly outlandish, but the kernel of truth at the center remained.

When Eleanor awoke the next morning, her head pounding and her mouth feeling like it was stuffed with cotton, her first coherent thought was, "Oh God, what did we do?"

But as the fog of her hangover slowly lifted, fragments of the night before came floating back. The laughter, the dreams, and the sense of possibility seemed to fill the room. And underneath it all, a feeling she hadn't experienced in far too long – excitement for the future.

Curt groaned beside her, throwing an arm over his eyes. "Please tell me we didn't actually decide to turn the Airbnb into a combination bakery-art center."

Eleanor chuckled, then winced at the pain in her head. "No, I think that idea came after we finished the Jack Daniels and moved on to that ancient bottle of rum."

They lay in silence for a while, both lost in thought. Finally, Eleanor spoke. "You know, beneath all the crazy drunk talk... I think we might have stumbled onto something."

Curt peeked out from under his arm. "Yeah?"

"Yeah," Eleanor said, sitting up slowly. "I mean, not the part about you becoming a master baker. But... the art center. The more I think about it, the more right it feels."

A slow smile spread across Curt's face. "I was hoping you'd say that. Because I've been lying here thinking that maybe it's time I looked into some small business classes."

Eleanor's heart swelled. "Really? You'd consider leaving the firm?"

"Consider it?" Curt sat up, taking her hand. "El, I haven't felt this excited about anything work-related in years. If you're willing to take a leap, so am I."

As they shared a tender, if slightly nauseous, kiss, Eleanor felt a profound sense of gratitude. For Joni and her wild story, for Curt and his unwavering support, and yes, even for Jack Daniels and its unlikely role as a catalyst for change.

Later that day, as they nursed their hangovers and began to sketch out more concrete plans, Eleanor insisted on making one stop.

The bell above Joni's Hardware chimed as they entered, Pearl babbling happily in her stroller.

Joni looked up from the counter, a knowing grin spreading across her face as she took in their haggard appearance. "Well, well, well. Looks like somebody had themselves a little 'vision quest' last night."

Eleanor laughed, ignoring the throb in her head. "Let's just say we took your story to heart. Also, thank you. For sharing it, I mean. It helped more than you know."

Joni's expression softened. "Glad to hear it, sugar. So, what can I help y'all with today? More home repair adventures?"

Eleanor and Curt exchanged a glance, then turned back to Joni with matching grins.

"Actually," Curt said, "we were hoping you might have some advice on how to start a small business..."

As Joni's booming laugh filled the store, Eleanor felt a sense of peace settle over her. The road ahead would be challenging, full of uncertainties and obstacles. But for the first time in a long while, she felt like she was on the right path. And honestly, that was worth any hangover.

Act 3. The Ponderance: In Vino Veritas

In the bustling streets of ancient Rome, a phrase was whispered among philosophers and revelers alike: "In vino veritas" – in wine, there is truth. This age-old adage has survived the centuries, inviting us to explore the complex relationship between altered states of consciousness and our quest for clarity and self-discovery.

The Romans weren't the first to notice the tongue-loosening effects of alcohol, but they certainly gave it a catchy name. "In vino veritas" speaks to the lowering of inhibitions and the revealing of one's true nature under the influence. But is there wisdom in this wine-soaked approach to truth-seeking?

While the Romans turned to wine, other cultures have long used various means to alter consciousness in pursuit of insight:

Native American vision quests often involve fasting and isolation in nature

Amazonian shamans use ayahuasca in ceremonial settings

Ancient Greek oracles inhaled vapors at Delphi to induce prophetic states

These practices share a common thread: the belief that stepping outside our normal state of mind can offer unique perspectives and truths.

There's no denying that lowered inhibitions can lead to startling honesty. How many of us have witnessed (or been) the person at a party who suddenly becomes a fountain of long-held secrets? But this "truth" comes at a cost:

1. Impaired judgment can lead to regrettable decisions

2. The clarity felt in the moment may not stand up to sober scrutiny

3. Reliance on substances for insight can become a dangerous crutch

So how do we reconcile this ancient wisdom with our contemporary understanding of psychology and decision-making? Perhaps the key lies not in the substance itself but in the state it induces:

Vulnerability

Openness to new ideas

Willingness to confront difficult truths

Fortunately, we don't need to reach for the wine bottle to achieve these states. Consider these alternative approaches to your personal vision quest:

1. Meditation and mindfulness practices
2. Journaling and self-reflection
3. Deep conversations with trusted friends
4. Immersion in nature
5. Engaging in creative pursuits

As we navigate the complexities of the modern world, the allure of "in vino veritas" remains. It speaks to our deep-seated desire to see clearly, to know ourselves truly, and to make decisions with conviction.

While we may not advocate for wine-fueled vision quests, we can certainly raise a glass to the timeless human pursuit of truth and self-discovery. May your own journey be rich with insight, whether it comes from a bottle of wine or a moment of quiet reflection.

Remember, the most profound truths often come not from external substances but from within ourselves – when we have the courage to look honestly and the wisdom to listen carefully.

As we come to the end of our journey through Savannah's whiskey-tinged tale of transformation, it's worth pausing to reflect on the unexpected wisdom found at the bottom of a glass.

Joni's hardware store revelation, Eleanor and Curt's drunken dreaming session, and even the ancient Romans' belief in "in vino veritas" all point to a universal truth: inspiration can strike in the most unlikely of places. But perhaps it's not about the Jack and Coke, the wine, or any other substance. Maybe it's about creating a space—mental or physical—where we allow ourselves to dream big, to be vulnerable, and to confront the truths we've been avoiding in our day-to-day lives.

The real magic doesn't lie in the alcohol, but in the courage it sometimes lends us to ask the big questions: Who am I? What do I really want? What would I do if I weren't afraid?

As you sip your own Jack and Coke (or iced tea, or kombucha, or whatever your drink of choice may be), remember that the path to self-discovery and fulfillment isn't always straight or conventional. Sometimes it winds through a hardware store in Savannah, a late-night conversation on a hardwood floor, or even a moment of quiet reflection in your favorite chair.

The key is to remain open to these moments of clarity, wherever they may find you. And when they do, have the courage to listen—really listen—to what your heart is telling you. Because at the end of the day, the most potent mix isn't Jack and Coke, but passion and purpose.

So here's to the dreamers, the risk-takers, and the late-night philosophers. May we all find our true calling, whether it comes to us in a vision, a drunken epiphany, or a quiet moment of reflection. And may we have the courage to pursue it, no matter how unconventional the path seems.

Remember, life is too short for watered-down dreams. So raise your glass—be it filled with whiskey or wisdom—and toast to the beautiful, messy, inspiring journey of finding your place in the world. After all, the best stories, like the best cocktails, are often a mix of the unexpected.

Cheers to your next adventure, whatever form it may take. It may be as bold and satisfying as the first sip of perfectly mixed Jack and Coke.

2

BACKROADS AND BITTERS

Act 1. The Spirits: Sidecar

The most memorable experiences in the art of mixology, as in life, often arise from unexpected combinations. As we embark on crafting the perfect Sidecar - a cocktail that balances the warmth of cognac, the brightness of citrus, and the sweetness of orange liqueur - we're reminded of how life's journey can take us down unfamiliar paths, leading to discoveries that transform us in ways we never anticipated. Just as each ingredient in the Sidecar plays a crucial role in creating a harmonious whole, every stop on a journey, no matter how small or seemingly insignificant, contributes to the rich tapestry of our experiences. This is the story of Tyler, a man whose unplanned detour off the beaten path led him to concoct a life as complex, balanced, and satisfying as the classic cocktail we're about to prepare.

As the evening settles in and the warm glow of your study lamp creates a cozy ambiance, you find yourself craving a cocktail that's both sophisticated and timeless. In an instant, the answer comes to you: a classic sidecar.

You begin by selecting an elegant coupe glass from your collection. Its shallow, broad bowl promises to showcase the drink's rich amber hue perfectly. You place it in the freezer for a quick chill while you gather your ingredients.

First, you reach for your cocktail shaker. The weight in your hand feels reassuring as you fill it with ice cubes, their crystalline surfaces catching the light.

Now for the sidecar's holy trinity. You start with cognac, the soul of the drink. As you uncork the bottle, the rich aroma of aged grapes fills the air. You pour two ounces into the shaker, and the amber liquid glides smoothly over the ice.

Next comes the Cointreau. Its clear appearance belies the intense orange flavor within. You measure out one ounce, then add it to the cognac. The citrus scent mingles with the cognac's warmth, creating an intoxicating bouquet.

Finally, you pick up a plump, ripe lemon. With deft movements, you slice it in half and squeeze one ounce of fresh juice into the shaker. The bright, zesty aroma cuts through the sweetness, promising to bring balance to your creation.

With all the ingredients assembled, you secure the lid on your shaker. In one fluid motion, you begin to shake. The ice rattles rhythmically as you move, chilling the liquors and melding their flavors into a harmonious blend. The shaker grows cold in your hands, frosting over slightly—a promise of the cool refreshment within.

After a vigorous shake, it's time for the reveal. You retrieve your chilled coupe glass from the freezer, its surface misty with frost. With practiced ease, you double-strain the cocktail into the waiting glass. The liquid pours out smoothly and clearly; its color is a perfect amber that catches the warm light of your study.

For the finishing touch, you decide to add a sugared rim. You run a lemon wedge around the top edge of the glass and dip the lip gently into a saucer of fine sugar. The crystals cling to the glass, forming a delicate, sparkling border.

You step back to admire your handiwork. The sidecar stands before you, elegant and inviting. Its color reminds you of aged bourbon, while the sugared rim adds a touch of frosted elegance.

As you lift the glass to your lips, the aroma hits you first - a complex blend of cognac's warmth, orange's sweetness, and lemon's brightness. The first sip is a revelation. The cognac provides a smooth, rich base, while the Cointreau adds depth and sweetness. The lemon juice brings a perfect tartness that balances the drink, while the sugared rim adds a delightful contrast of texture and sweetness.

In this moment, you realize you've crafted more than just a cocktail. This Sidecar is a sensory journey—a perfect balance of flavors that harkens back to the golden age of cocktails. It's a reminder of why this drink has stood the test of time, delighting palates for nearly a century.

As you settle into your favorite leather armchair, Sidecar in hand, you can't help but feel a sense of connection to the past. This isn't just a drink - it's a piece of cocktail history, a toast to the art of mixology. With each sip, you savor not just the flavors but the moment itself, perfectly captured in a glass as timeless and sophisticated as the evening that inspired it.

I'd like to share the real-life experience that inspired me to write the following tale. Let me set the scene for you:

I vividly recall that crisp Georgia evening. I had just wrapped up a fancy meeting in Thomasville and was racing back to Atlanta for a board meeting. Armed with nothing but a new GPS and misplaced confidence, I decided to take a shortcut. That decision would prove to be a pivotal moment in my life.

After one missed turn, I found myself on a dark country road. An unfortunate encounter with a fox later, I ended up at a backwater gas station, washing blood off my hands and experiencing what I can only describe as an existential crisis. Standing there, covered in dirt and engine grease, I made a vow to myself: No more GPS. No more shortcuts. No more missing the journey to the destination.

In that moment, I made what felt like the only rational choice. I bought a map—the Georgia Gazette, to be exact. Then and there, I decided to make it my personal mission to visit every single town listed in that dog-eared atlas.

That impulsive decision changed everything for me. Through this journey, I discovered a Georgia—and a version of myself—that I never knew existed.

This personal experience became the foundation for the story I've written, blending my real-life adventure with fictional elements to create a narrative that I hope captures the transformative power of stepping off the beaten path.

Act 2. The Tale: The Fox and a Map

The GPS said 'recalculating' for the hundredth time as Tyler's tie grew tighter around his neck, much like the noose of civilization he was inadvertently slipping out of. He'd left the air-conditioned comfort of the Thomasville conference room just three hours ago, but it felt like he'd driven into another world entirely.

"Recalculating," chirped the robotic voice, for what seemed like the hundredth time. Tyler sighed, loosening his tie and unbuttoning his collar. The paved road had given way to gravel, then to hard-packed dirt. Now, endless rows of corn stretched out on either side, their green stalks swaying gently in the late afternoon breeze.

He was about to admit defeat and turn back when a flash of russet fur darted across the road. Tyler slammed on the brakes, but it was too late. A sickening thud, followed by a horrible grinding noise, told him all he needed to know.

"No, no, no," he muttered, climbing out of the truck. The acrid smell of burnt rubber mixed with something metallic – blood. Tyler's stomach churned as he approached the front of the vehicle. A fox was tangled in the fan belt, his eyes wide and glassy.

For a moment, Tyler just stood there, the reality of the situation slowly sinking in. In Georgia, he was lost in the middle of nowhere, with a mangled animal in his engine and not a soul in sight. His phone, predictably, showed no signal.

With a deep breath, Tyler steeled himself for what he had to do. Rolling up his sleeves, he reached into the engine compartment. The fox's fur was still warm, its limbs limp as he tried to extricate it from the mechanical grip of the fan belt. As he worked, blood smeared across his hands and white dress shirt, and the Georgia heat intensified the coppery smell.

After what felt like an eternity, Tyler managed to free the animal's remains. He laid it gently in the cornfield, murmuring a quiet apology to the creature whose life he'd inadvertently ended. Turning back to his truck, he grimaced at the sight of himself in the side mirror – disheveled, sweat-stained, and covered in blood.

As Tyler climbed back into the driver's seat, a new determination took hold. He'd find his way back to civilization, clean himself up, and never take another backroad shortcut again. Little did he know that this gruesome detour was about to set him on a journey that would change his life forever.

The truck's engine sputtered and coughed as Tyler pulled into the gravel lot of the Piney Woods Diner. The neon "Open" sign flickered weakly in the twilight, a beacon of civilization in the sea of rural Georgia. Tyler glanced at his blood-stained reflection in the rearview mirror and swallowed hard. He had no choice; he needed directions and possibly a mechanic.

As he pushed open the diner's door, a small bell chimed overhead. The handful of patrons inside fell silent, all eyes turning to the disheveled stranger. Tyler felt their stares burning into him as he made his way to the counter, leaving a trail of dusty, blood-speckled footprints in his wake.

"Evenin'," drawled the waitress, her plastered-on smile faltering as she took in Tyler's appearance. "You, uh... you alright there, hon?"

Tyler nodded, perhaps a bit too vigorously. "Yes, ma'am. I just had a bit of car trouble down the road. Hit a fox." The words tumbled out, and his voice was higher than usual. "I don't suppose you could point me towards a mechanic?"

The waitress – Dolores, according to her name tag – eyed him suspiciously. "Nearest garage is closed for the night. You're welcome to use our phone to call a tow, though."

As Dolores turned to fetch the phone, Tyler became acutely aware of the whispered conversations behind him. He caught fragments – "covered in blood," "city folk," "up to no good" – that sent his paranoia into overdrive.

An older man at the end of the counter, his weathered

face partially hidden by the brim of a John Deere cap, spoke up. "You said you hit a fox? Where 'bouts?"

"I... I'm not sure exactly," Tyler stammered. "Some dirt road off the highway. There was a cornfield..."

"Hmm," the man grunted, exchanging glances with a younger man who could have been his son. "Lotta cornfields 'round here."

Tyler's heart raced. Did they think he was lying? That he'd done something worse than hit an animal? He could almost hear their unspoken accusations.

Dolores returned with an ancient rotary phone, plunking it down on the counter. "Here you go, sugar. You want some coffee while you wait?"

Tyler nodded gratefully, fumbling with the unfamiliar phone as he dialed the tow company's number. As he waited for an answer, he couldn't shake the feeling of being watched. Every clink of silverware and murmured word seemed to carry sinister undertones.

The tow truck, he was told, wouldn't arrive for at least two hours. Tyler slumped on his stool, cradling the mug of lukewarm coffee Dolores had poured him. He'd have to wait it out, marinating in his own discomfort and the townsfolk's suspicion.

As the minutes ticked by agonizingly slow, Tyler's imagination ran wild. What if they called the police? What if they decided to take matters into their own hands, assuming he was some kind of murderer? He'd heard stories about outsiders in small Southern towns...

Just as Tyler was considering making a run for it, the bell above the door chimed again. In walked a man in grease-stained overalls, wiping his hands on a red rag.

"You the fella with the truck trouble?" he asked, his voice booming in the quiet diner.

Tyler nodded, relief washing over him. "Yes, that's me."

The mechanic looked him up and down, taking in the blood-stained clothes. A knowing smile crept across his face. "Hit an animal, did ya? C'mon, let's take a look at that truck of yours."

As Tyler followed the mechanic out, he felt the weight of the diner patrons' stares lifting. Outside, the night air cooled against his skin, and he finally allowed himself to breathe.

The mechanic, introducing himself as Hank, popped the hood of Tyler's truck and whistled low. "Yep, that critter did a number on your fan belt. Lucky you made it this far." He glanced at Tyler, a hint of amusement in his eyes. "You know, you coulda just told folks inside what happened. We may be a small town, but we ain't all gossips and judgmental folk."

Tyler felt his face flush with embarrassment. "I... I guess I let my imagination get the better of me."

Hank chuckled, already setting to work on the engine. "Happens to the best of us, son. Especially when you're lost in unfamiliar territory." He paused, looking up at Tyler. "Tell you what. While I'm fixing this, why don't you go back inside and clean yourself up a bit? Might make you feel more human. And who knows, you might even find the folks in there ain't so scary after all."

With a sheepish nod, Tyler turned back towards the diner. As he reached for the door, he hesitated, then squared his shoulders. Maybe it was time to face his fears—and – of these people – head-on. After all, he had nothing to hide. Just a city boy, lost in the country, with a story to tell.

Little did Tyler know, this night – with its fear, embarrassment, and unexpected kindness – would be the first of many encounters that would reshape his understanding of rural Georgia and its people.

The next morning, Tyler found himself back on the

highway, heading towards Atlanta. His truck hummed smoothly, thanks to Hank's late-night repairs. As he drove, Tyler couldn't shake the memory of the previous evening – the fear, the paranoia, and ultimately, the unexpected kindness he'd encountered.

He pulled into a rest stop just outside of Macon, stretching his legs and breathing in the crisp morning air. Inside the visitor center, a rack of maps and brochures caught his eye. Among them was a thick, detailed map titled "Georgia Gazette: Every Town, Every Road."

Tyler picked it up, thumbing through the pages. It was comprehensive, showing not just the major cities and highways but every tiny hamlet and back road across the state. As he traced the winding lines with his finger, something stirred in him.

Back in his truck, Tyler spread the map across the passenger seat. He thought about his job – endless meetings, PowerPoint presentations, and stuffy conference rooms. Then he remembered the open road, the cornfields, and even the ill-fated fox. There had been fear, yes, but also a sense of adventure he hadn't felt in years.

An idea began to form—crazy and impulsive yet oddly appealing. What if, instead of just driving from one big city to another for work, he took the time to explore? To see every little town, every forgotten corner of Georgia?

Tyler pulled out a pen and, before he could talk himself out of it, circled Thomasville – where this whole adventure had begun. Then, with a sense of purpose he hadn't felt in years, he began plotting a route that would take him to every named place on the map.

As he merged back onto the highway, Tyler's mind raced with possibilities. He'd need to rearrange his work schedule, maybe even take some time off. But the thought of discovering the real Georgia – not just the Atlanta boardrooms and Savannah tourist traps – filled him with excitement.

His first stop was a tiny place called Benevolence, a speck on the map that he might have missed if he hadn't been looking for it. As Tyler turned off the main road, he felt a familiar apprehension. But this time, instead of fear, he felt a thrill of anticipation.

Benevolence turned out to be little more than a crossroads with a general store, a church, and a handful of houses. But as Tyler parked in front of the store, an old man in overalls nodded a greeting from his rocking chair on the porch.

"Mornin'," the man called out. "You look a mite lost, son."

Tyler smiled, thinking of how lost he'd been just yesterday. "Not lost, sir. Just exploring. I'm trying to visit every town in Georgia."

The old man's eyebrows shot up, then he let out a hearty laugh. "Every town? Well, you've got your work cut out for you, ain't ya? Come on in, let me tell you 'bout Benevolence. Ain't much to tell, mind you, but it's home."

As Tyler followed the man into the store, he felt a weight lifting from his shoulders. This was what he'd been missing – genuine connections, real stories, a Georgia beyond the highways and skyscrapers.

Over the next few hours, Tyler learned more about Benevolence than he ever thought possible. The old man – Mr. Johnson, as he introduced himself – regaled him with tales of the town's founding, pointed out centuries-old trees, and introduced him to every person who came into the store.

By the time Tyler left, the sun was setting, painting the sky in brilliant oranges and pinks. He hadn't made it far on his journey, but he felt like he'd traveled a lifetime from the stressed, paranoid man he'd been yesterday.

As he drove towards his next destination, Tyler felt a sense of peace settle over him. He glanced at the map, which was now marked with a bold check next to Benevolence. One down, hundreds to go. But for the first time in years, Tyler wasn't racing towards a destination. He was enjoying the journey.

Little did he know, this impulsive decision would lead him to discover not just the hidden gems of Georgia but also parts of himself he never knew existed. The road ahead was long, winding, and full of surprises – just the way Tyler was beginning to like it.

Over the next few months, Tyler's map became a patchwork of checkmarks and scribbled notes. Each town, no matter how small, left its mark on him. Here are a few of the most memorable encounters:

Talking Rock, GA

The name alone had intrigued Tyler, and he wasn't disappointed. As he pulled into the tiny town, he spotted a group of elderly men sitting in rocking chairs outside the local barbershop. They waved him over, and Tyler soon found himself caught up in a tradition as old as the town itself - the "Talking Rock Talk."

"You see that boulder over yonder?" One man, who identified himself as Clarence, inquired. "Legend has it, if you put your ear to it at midnight during a full moon, you can hear the whispers of Cherokee spirits."

Tyler spent the afternoon listening to tales that blurred the line between history and folklore. When he finally left, his head was spinning with stories of Civil War ghosts, hidden moonshine stills, and secret Underground Railroad passages.

Hopeulikit, GA

Tyler couldn't resist stopping in a town with such an unusual name. The mystery was solved when he met Mabel, the 90-year-old proprietor of the town's only store.

"My grandpappy founded this place," she explained, her eyes twinkling. "He was courtin' my grandma, and every time she'd visit, he'd say, 'Hope you like it!' It became a sort of joke between them, and when they settled here, well, the name just stuck."

Tyler left Hopeulikit with a jar of Mabel's famous peach preserves and a renewed appreciation for the power of love and humor in shaping a community.

Between, GA

Tyler couldn't help but chuckle at the town sign: "Welcome to Between - You're Here!" He soon learned that the town's location - precisely between Athens and Atlanta - was a source of both pride and frustration for its residents.

"We're always caught in the middle," said Joe, the owner of the local diner. "UGA fans on one side, Georgia Tech on the other. Presidential candidates stop here to prove they care about 'middle America.' Heck, we even had to settle a dispute about which time zone we're in!"

Tyler left Between with a deeper understanding of the complex identities that small towns often grapple with, caught between larger, competing influences.

Climax, GA

Despite its suggestive name, Climax turned out to be a quiet farming community. However, it was here that Tyler had one of his most profound experiences.

He arrived just as the town was preparing for its annual Swine Time Festival. Before he knew it, he was roped into helping set up for the event, working alongside locals to erect tents and string up lights.

As night fell, the festival came to life. Tyler found himself judging a greased pig-catching contest, tapping his foot to local bluegrass bands and sampling every variety of barbecue imaginable.

In the early hours of the morning, as the festival wound down, Tyler sat on a hay bale with Mary Ellen, an 80-year-old former schoolteacher.

"You know," she said, her voice soft with memories, "I've seen this festival every year of my life. Watched it grow from a little community picnic to... well, this." She gestured at the fairgrounds that surrounded them. "But it's not about the size. It's about the people. This is where we come together, where we remember who we are."

Tyler nodded, comprehension dawning. In Climax, he realized, he'd seen the heart of what made these small towns special. It wasn't just quirky names or interesting histories. It was the sense of community, the shared traditions, and the way people came together.

As he drove away the next morning, adding another check to his ever-filling map, Tyler felt a profound sense of gratitude. He'd set out to explore Georgia, but he was discovering so much more - about the state, its people, and himself.

Little did he know, his journey was far from over, and the most impactful encounters were yet to come.

As the months rolled by, Tyler's journey through Georgia's small towns began to change him in ways he never expected. The polished business executive was giving way to a more relaxed, curious, and open-minded individual. However, this transformation didn't come without its challenges.

One crisp autumn morning, Tyler found himself in Irwinville, the site where Jefferson Davis was captured at the end of the Civil War. As he explored the small museum, he overheard a heated discussion between two locals about how the war should be remembered.

For the first time, Tyler realized the complexity of Southern history and identity. He'd always seen things in black and white, but now he was learning to appreciate the shades of gray. This newfound perspective made him uncomfortable at times, challenging his preconceptions and forcing him to confront difficult truths about the state he was growing to love.

In Chula, a tiny agricultural town, Tyler's city slicker status became a liability. His truck got stuck in the mud on a back road, and he had no idea how to get it out. A local farmer named Jeb came to his rescue, teaching Tyler how to use a winch and giving him a crash course in navigating rural roads.

"City boy like you's got no business out here alone," Jeb had said, not unkindly. "But I reckon you're learning. That's something, at least."

The incident left Tyler feeling humbled but determined. He realized how much he still had to learn about this world he was exploring. That night, in his motel room, he ordered a set of topographical maps and started studying the terrain of the areas he planned to visit next.

As winter approached, Tyler faced another challenge: loneliness. The constant travel and brief encounters, while exciting, left little room for deep connections. During a surprise snowstorm in Warthen, he found himself the only guest at a small bed and breakfast.

The owner, a widow named Grace, sensed his melancholy and invited him to join her family for dinner. Surrounded by the warmth of their home and their easy laughter, Tyler felt a pang of longing for the life he'd left behind.

"You know, honey," Grace said as she handed him a slice of pecan pie, "it's good to wander, to find yourself. But don't forget to let yourself be found, too."

Her words stuck with Tyler long after he left Warthen. He began to make a conscious effort to stay in touch with the people he met, sending postcards and making phone calls. Slowly, he was building a network of friends across the state, turning his solo journey into a shared experience.

In Tallapoosa, Tyler faced perhaps his biggest challenge yet. He arrived just as the town was grappling with the closure of its main employer, a textile mill. The mood was somber, and for the first time, Tyler felt like an intruder, his presence an uncomfortable reminder of the outside world that seemed to have forgotten them.

But as he spent time in the town, listening to people's stories and concerns, something shifted. Tyler found himself using his business knowledge to help a group of former mill workers draft a proposal for a small business incubator. He spent late nights poring over budget sheets and making calls to his old contacts in Atlanta.

When he finally left Tallapoosa two weeks later, the incubator project was underway, and Tyler had gained a new perspective on his skills and how he could use them to make a difference.

This experience marked a turning point in Tyler's journey. He was no longer just an observer, but an active partici-pant in the communities he visited. He began to see each town not just as a checkpoint on his map but as a living, breathing entity with its own challenges and opportunities.

As spring bloomed across Georgia, Tyler looked at himself in the rearview mirror of his now-well-traveled truck. His hair was longer, and his skin had tanned from days spent outdoors. But the biggest change was in his eyes; they sparkled with a newfound purpose and understanding.

He picked up his much-annotated Georgia Gazette map, running his fingers over the familiar creases. More than half the towns were now checked off, each mark representing not just a visit but a lesson learned, a connection made, and a piece of himself discovered.

Tyler realized that somewhere along the backroads of Georgia, he'd found more than just small towns. He'd found a new way of seeing the world, and perhaps more impor-tantly, a new way of seeing himself.

As he started the engine and pulled onto the road towards his next destination, Tyler felt a sense of anticipa-tion. He didn't know what challenges or growth opportuni-ties awaited him, but for the first time in his life, he was truly ready to face them.

As Tyler's journey neared its end, he found himself in Savannah, the last major stop on his tour of Georgia. The historic city, with its Spanish moss-draped squares and ante-bellum architecture, felt like a fitting place to reflect on his odyssey through the backroads of the South.

He settled into a seat at the bar of a trendy craft cocktail spot, a far cry from the small-town dives and rural watering holes he'd frequented over the past year. The bartender, noticing Tyler's weathered appearance and faraway look, struck up a conversation.

"What'll it be, stranger?"

Tyler smiled, bringing back memories. "What's your most complex cocktail? Something with layers, something that tells a story."

Intrigued, the bartender nodded and set to work. Minutes later, he presented Tyler with a rich, amber-colored drink in a rocks glass, garnished with a twist of orange peel and a sprig of fresh herbs.

"I call this one 'Georgia on My Mind,'" the bartender said. "It's a base of peach-infused bourbon, layered with homemade corn whiskey, a touch of sorghum syrup, and a dash of pecan bitters. Give it a try."

Tyler lifted the glass to his nose, inhaling deeply before taking a sip. The flavors exploded on his palate, each one evoking a memory from his travels.

The sweet burn of the bourbon took him back to a moonshine tasting in the North Georgia mountains, where an old-timer had shown him the art of distilling in a hidden cave, the spirit as clear and potent as mountain spring water.

The subtle corn notes reminded him of Leary, the "Vitamin B Capital of the World," where he'd participated in a corn shucking contest and learned about the town's unique claim to fame.

The sorghum's earthy sweetness transported him to Blairsville, where he'd helped harvest sorghum cane and watched as it was pressed and boiled down into syrup, the air thick with the scent of caramelizing sugar.

The nutty undertones from the pecan bitters brought back memories of Camilla, where he'd joined in the annual Gnat Days festival, competing in a pecan pie eating contest and learning about the town's agricultural heritage.

And the fresh herbal aroma from the garnish reminded

him of the community gardens he'd helped plant in towns struggling with food insecurity, the simple act of nurturing life from the Georgia soil connecting him to generations of farmers and gardeners.

As Tyler savored the drink, he pulled out his well-worn map of Georgia. Nearly every town was now checked off, each mark representing not just a visit but a story, a connection, a piece of himself left behind, and something new gained in return.

"You look like a man with stories to tell," the bartender observed, cleaning a glass.

Tyler nodded, a slow smile spreading across his face. "More than I ever thought possible. I set out to see every town in Georgia, but somewhere along the way, I found something more."

He took another sip of his drink, letting the complex flavors mingle on his tongue. "You know, this cocktail... it's a lot like my journey. Each ingredient is distinct, but they come together to create something greater than the sum of its parts. Sweet, bitter, strong, subtle... just like the people and places I've encountered."

The bartender leaned in, intrigued. "Sounds like quite an adventure. Care to share some of those stories?"

Tyler glanced at his watch, then back at his map. He now had all the time in the world and a heart full of tales to tell. "Well," he began, settling into his seat, "it all started with a fox and a cornfield..."

As Tyler recounted his adventures, he realized that his journey through Georgia's small towns had changed him profoundly. The ambitious executive who had set out a year ago was gone, replaced by a man who understood the value of community, the richness of diversity, and the profound stories hidden in the most unassuming places.

The night wore on, and Tyler's stories flowed as freely as the expertly crafted cocktails. Each sip and story shared reaffirmed his connection to the state he had come to love, not just for its picturesque landscapes or quaint towns, but for the spirit of its people and the unexpected wisdom found on its dusty backroads.

As last call approached, Tyler knew his journey wasn't really ending. It was evolving into something new—something that would allow him to give back to the communities that had given him so much. The road ahead was uncertain, but for the first time in his life, Tyler was excited about the unknown.

He raised his glass in a silent toast—to Georgia, to its small towns, and to the transformative power of taking the road less traveled.

Act 3. The Ponderance: The Lost Art of Map Reading

I have found myself reflecting on an unexpected revelation from my cross-country trip in 2022: the dying art of map reading. What began as a simple tool for navigation became a lens through which I observed a subtle but significant shift in our society.

Picture this: You're standing on a street corner in a small town, somewhere in the heart of America. You've pulled out your trusty paper map, trying to get your bearings. You spot a local and decide to ask for help. "Excuse me, could you show me where we are on this map?" The response? A blank stare, followed by an apologetic shrug. This scene played out more times than I can count during my journey, especially with younger folks who seemed utterly lost when faced with a folded piece of paper covered in lines and symbols.

It struck me then - we're losing something fundamental. In our rush to embrace the convenience of GPS and smartphone navigation, we've inadvertently let slip a skill that connects us more intimately with our surroundings. There's a world of difference between following turn-by-turn directions and truly understanding the lay of the land.

But it wasn't just the declining map-reading skills that caught my attention. Midway through my trip, I found myself in need of a replacement map. To my surprise, finding a paper map became an adventure in itself. Gas stations, convenience stores, and even bookshops—places that once dedicated entire racks to maps—now looked at me quizzically when I made my request. It was as if I'd asked for a telegraph machine or a sundial.

This scarcity of paper maps raises an interesting question: Are we becoming too reliant on technology for something as fundamental as knowing where we are and how to get where we're going?

Don't get me wrong - I appreciate the convenience of digital navigation as much as anyone. But there's something to be said for the freedom a paper map provides. It allows you to see the big picture, to make spontaneous decisions, and to choose the scenic route over the fastest one.

Which brings me to another point of reflection: Who's to say that the algorithm knows the best route for me? Sometimes, the journey itself is more important than the time it takes to reach the destination. A winding road through a picturesque valley might add an hour to your trip, but it could also add a lifetime of memories.

As I traveled across the USA, map in hand, I realized that I wasn't just navigating roads and highways. I was navigating the changing landscape of how we interact with the world. The paper map, with its creases and coffee stains, became a symbol of a more engaged, more intentional way of traveling—and perhaps of living.

So, the next time you're planning a trip, consider picking up a paper map. Spread it out on your kitchen table. Trace potential routes with your finger. Let your imagination wander along those thin lines that crisscross the page. You might just find that the journey begins long before you start your engine.

And who knows? You might discover a skill you never knew you were missing, or rediscover one you'd forgotten you had. In a world that's constantly pushing us to move faster, to be more efficient, perhaps there's value in occasionally taking the long way round - guided by nothing more than a folded piece of paper and your own sense of adventure.

As the last drops of the "Georgia on My Mind" cocktail lingered on Tyler's palate, he realized that his journey through the backroads of Georgia had been more than just a tour of small towns. It had been a rediscovery of the lost art of navigation – not just of roads but of life itself.

Like the complex layers of the cocktail, each town, each encounter, and each wrong turn added depth and richness to his experience. The peach-infused bourbon reminded him of the sweetness found in unexpected places. The corn whiskey echoed the rawness of authentic connections. The sorghum syrup represented the slow, patient process of personal growth. And the pecan bitters? They were the challenges that made the journey worthwhile.

Tyler thought back to that first night, lost on a dirt road with nothing but a malfunctioning GPS. How different things might have been if he'd had a paper map from the start. But then again, would he have embarked on this transformative journey if he hadn't first been truly, utterly lost?

As he folded up his well-worn, annotation-filled map of Georgia, Tyler understood that he had learned to read more than just roads and rivers. He had learned to read the stories written in the faces of small-town folks, the history etched into the landscapes, and the potential hidden in overlooked places.

The bartender, sensing the weight of Tyler's reflections, topped off his glass. "To the road less traveled," he said with a knowing smile.

Tyler raised his glass in return. "And to the maps that show us the way – especially when we choose to ignore them."

As he sipped the last of his drink, Tyler knew that while his Georgia odyssey might be ending, a new journey was just beginning. He had a whole country to explore, a thousand more stories to uncover, and countless roads – both on maps and off – yet to travel.

With a career in the rearview mirror and an open road ahead, Tyler stepped out into the Savannah night, ready to let the next adventure find him. After all, sometimes the best destinations are the ones you never planned to reach, guided by nothing more than a folded piece of paper and an insatiable curiosity for what lies just beyond the next turn.

3

PURPLE HAZE AND PASAQUAN

Act 1. The Spirits: Purple Haze

As the Purple Haze cocktail swirls in its glass, a kaleidoscope of indigo and lavender mirrors the vibrant, psychedelic world of Pasaquan. Just as the drink blends vodka, Chambord, and blue curaçao into a mesmerizing concoction, so too did Eddie Owens Martin, better known as St. EOM, blend art, spirituality, and madness into his own intoxicating vision. Both the cocktail and the man are testaments to the transformative power of creativity, turning the ordinary into something extraordinary and inviting us to see the world through a lens tinted by imagination and wonder.

As the evening sky deepens into twilight, you find yourself drawn to create a cocktail that captures the mystique of the fading light. Your mind conjures the perfect choice: a Purple Haze, a drink as enchanting as its name suggests.

You begin by selecting a tall, slender Collins glass. Its crystal-clear surface promises to showcase the magical hues of your creation. You fill it with ice, the cubes tinkling against the glass like wind chimes in a gentle breeze.

First comes the vodka, which forms the foundation of your Purple Haze. You choose a premium bottle whose contents are as clear as mountain spring water. With a steady hand, you pour a generous measure over the ice, watching as it cascades down, embracing the frozen cubes.

Next, you reach for the star of the show—the chambord. As you uncork the distinctive globe-shaped bottle, the rich aroma of black raspberries fills the air. You pour the liqueur slowly, watching as it sinks through the vodka and creates mesmerizing purple swirls in its wake.

Now for the blue curaçao, the magical ingredient that will transform your drink into a true purple haze. Its vibrant blue color is a stark contrast to the deep red of the Chambord. As you add it to the mix, it creates a beautiful interplay of colors, like twilight clouds streaking across the sky.

To balance the sweetness and add a refreshing twist, you reach for a bottle of lemon-lime soda. As you pour it over the colorful mixture, it fizzes and bubbles, lifting the heavier liqueurs and creating a captivating gradient of purple hues.

With a long bar spoon, you give the drink a gentle stir, just enough to blend the flavors without losing the stunning color separation. The ice shifts and settles, chilling the mixture to perfection.

For the finishing touch, you select a plump, ripe blackberry and a twist of lemon peel. You carefully balance the blackberry on the glass's rim and drop the lemon twist into the drink, watching as it bobs and weaves through the purple liquid.

You step back to admire your handiwork. The Purple Haze stands before you, a visual masterpiece. Its layers of color shimmer in the dim light, from deep indigo at the bottom to a soft lavender at the top, crowned with the soda fizz.

As you lift the glass to your lips, the aroma hits you first —a complex bouquet of berries, citrus, and subtle herbal notes. The first sip is a revelation. The vodka provides a smooth backdrop, while the chambord and blue curaçao create a fruity, sweet melody on your tongue. The soda adds a refreshing effervescence, lifting and brightening the flavors.

In this moment, you realize you've created more than just a cocktail. This Purple Haze is a sensory journey, a perfect balance of flavors and visual appeal that captures the magic of twilight in a glass. It's a reminder of the art of mixology, how a few carefully chosen ingredients can come together to create something truly enchanting.

As you settle into your favorite spot on the balcony, Purple Haze in hand, you can't help but feel a sense of wonder. This isn't just a drink - it's a potion, a magical elixir that transforms an ordinary evening into something extraordinary. With each sip, you savor not just the flavors but the moment itself, perfectly captured in a glass as mysterious and beautiful as the purple haze of dusk.

In the end, the legacy of St. EOM, like the lingering taste of a Purple Haze cocktail, reminds us of the beauty found in the unconventional. Just as each sip of the drink reveals layers of flavor, each glimpse into Pasaquan uncovers layers of meaning and mystery. Both the cocktail and the artist invite us to embrace the unusual, find magic in the mundane, and create our own vibrant realities. As we raise our glasses, the purple liquid catching the light like the painted walls of Pasaquan, we toast to those visionaries who dare to mix the colors of their dreams into the canvas of the world, leaving behind a swirling, shimmering testament to the power of unfettered creativity. This is a tale that's been percolating in my mind since my days of working with endangered historic sites across the great state of Georgia. It's a story that emerged from whispers and fragments, local lore and legend, all centered around a remarkable place known as Pasaquan.

Picture this: a psychedelic oasis nestled in the heart of Buena Vista, Georgia, a place I encountered while working for the Georgia Trust. As a partner in the field, I was tasked with trying to save this endangered historic site, which had been left largely untouched since the death of its creator, St. EOM.

Before we dive into the story, let me paint a picture of the site's profound isolation. Imagine driving down a narrow, winding road, surrounded by dense Georgia pines that seem to whisper secrets of the past. The pavement gives way to gravel, then to dirt, as civilization fades in the rearview mirror. Minutes stretch into what feels like hours as you venture deeper into the rural heartland. Finally, around a bend, you catch your first glimpse of Pasaquan—a burst of color so unexpected in this sea of green that it almost seems like a mirage.

The site, when I first saw it, was a haunting blend of decay and defiant vibrancy. Weeds pushed through cracked concrete, and the once-brilliant paint was fading under the relentless Southern sun. Yet, even in its unrestored state, the power of St. EOM's vision was palpable. It was a place where art and madness intertwined, where visions became reality, and where one man's quest for meaning led to the creation of a truly otherworldly environment.

Our story takes us back to the sweltering summer of 1965, when the cicadas droned and the air hung thick with possibility. It's a tale of St. EOM, also known as Eddie Owens

Martin, a self-styled visionary who transformed his little patch of Georgia into a technicolor dreamland.

But this isn't just about art, folks. Oh no, we've got politics, we've got fortune-telling, we've got a dash of the counterculture, and maybe even a future president thrown into the mix. It's a quintessentially Southern Gothic tale, filled with larger-than-life characters and the kind of twists that could only happen in the backwoods of Georgia.

As I worked to help preserve this unique slice of American folk art history, I couldn't help but be drawn into the fascinating world of St. EOM and the legacy he left behind in this isolated corner of the South.

Act 2. The Tale: The Pasaquanian

In the sweltering heart of 1965 Georgia, where cicadas droned and conformity reigned, there stood a psychedelic oasis that defied reality itself. Welcome to Pasaquan, where a self-proclaimed visionary named St. EOM painted prophecies, hosted improbable guests, and danced on the razor's edge between genius and madness. When an ambitious politician and his wife stepped into this kaleidoscopic world seeking guidance, they had no idea their encounter with the eccentric fortune-teller would set in motion a journey that would lead all the way to the White House. Strap in for a tale that proves truth is stranger—and more colorful—than fiction.

The cicadas' relentless drone filled the thick, humid air of Buena Vista, Georgia. It was the summer of 1965, and the heat shimmered off the psychedelic murals that adorned Pasaquan's buildings. In the heart of this surreal oasis sat St. EOM, known to some as Eddie Owens Martin, hunched over a teacup on his colorfully painted porch.

His weathered hands, adorned with homemade rings and bangles, cradled the delicate china as he peered intently at the remaining leaves. The sweet scent of marijuana drifted from a rolled cigarette, balanced precariously on an ashtray fashioned from a hollowed-out gourd. St. EOM's long, unkempt beard and wild eyes gave him the appearance of a man caught between worlds – which, in many ways, he was.

"Well, I'll be damned," he muttered, his voice a gravelly drawl that betrayed both his Georgia

roots and the years he'd spent in the concrete jungle of New York City. "Looks like change is coming, and it ain't just the weather."

He set the cup down and leaned back in his hand-painted chair, letting his gaze wander over the vibrant landscape he'd created. Pasaquan was his masterpiece, a testament to the visions that had haunted him since his youth. It was also his sanctuary, a place where the judgmental whispers of Buena Vista's townsfolk couldn't reach him.

St. EOM chuckled to himself, remembering the faces of those proper Southern ladies and gentlemen when they'd first laid eyes on his creation. They'd called him mad, a disgrace to the community. But he knew better. He'd seen things they couldn't even imagine during his time up North.

His mind drifted back to the smoky nightclubs and lavish apartments of New York City. He'd never had a place to call his own there, but he'd never needed one. There was always another wealthy patron, another curious socialite eager to hear what the stars had in store for them. And if they wanted more than just a reading? Well, a man had to eat, didn't he?

Now, darling, you must understand that our dear St. EOM was no ordinary fortune-teller. Oh no, he was a veritable kaleidoscope of a man, as colorful and unpredictable as the swirling murals that adorned his peculiar kingdom. And on this particular sweltering Georgia afternoon, he was about to receive the most unlikely of visitors.

The shimmering heat of the Georgia summer hung heavy in the air as a gleaming 1950s Studebaker Commander kicked up a cloud of dust along the dirt road. Its sleek, bullet-nose design and distinctive wrap-around rear window cut an impressive figure against the rural land-scape. The car's whitewall tires crunched to a stop in front of Pasaquan's ornate gates.

From the radio drifted the Lyrics sung by Petula Clark, "So go downtown....Things will be great when you're down-town" . As the last notes faded, a lean, bespectacled man emerged from the driver's side, his eyes twinkling with a mix of curiosity and determination behind his glasses. A petite woman stepped out of the passenger door, her posture and poise exuding a quiet strength that matched the intensity of the summer heat.

St. EOM, observing the arrival from his colorful perch, felt a spark of recognition. He rose slowly, his own eccentric appearance in sharp contrast to the neat, pressed clothes of his visitors.

"Well, I'll be," St. EOM drawled, a hint of amusement in his voice. "If it isn't Jimmy Carter and his lovely wife paying a visit to my little slice of paradise."

Jimmy approached with an outstretched hand, his warm smile matching the sunny day. "Mr. Martin, I presume? I've heard quite a bit about your work here. It's a pleasure to finally see it in person."

"Honey, around here, it's St. EOM or nothing at all," he replied with a wink that made Rosalynn blush ever so slightly. Rosalynn stepped out, dressed elegantly in a sunny yellow dress. Her hands were covered by crisp white gloves, and her feet were adorned with matching white shoes. As they made their way through the psychedelic wonderland, Rosalynn couldn't help but gasp. "It's... it's..."

"Something else, ain't it?" St. EOM finished for her, a hint of pride in his voice. "Folks 'round here think I've lost my marbles. But sugar, you can't lose what you never had to begin with."

Jimmy chuckled, his eyes roving over the totemic sculptures and mandala-like designs. "It's certainly unique. But we're not here for the art, fascinating as it is."

"No, I reckon you're not," St. EOM agreed, ushering them into his reading room. The air was thick with incense and the unmistakable aroma of what the locals referred to as "grass."

Now, my dears, you might wonder what business an aspiring politician and his wife had with our eccentric artist. But in the South, even the most straight-laced have their secrets and superstitions. And Jimmy Carter, with his eyes on the governor's mansion, was no exception.

St. EOM settled them around a small table, its surface a swirl of painted constellations. With practiced hands, he prepared the tea, a blend of his own creation that smelled of jasmine and something... else. Something that made Rosalynn's eyes widen just a fraction.

As they drank, St. EOM regaled them with tales of his New York days. He spoke of nights at the Stonewall, of soirées with society's elite, and of a particular evenin with Truman Capote "You know," St. EOM mused, his eyes taking on a faraway look, "New York has its charms. But there's something about the South that calls to a person's soul. It's in the air, in the very soil."

Jimmy nodded with a thoughtful expression. "It's why

we're here, Mr. Mar- I mean, St. EOM. Georgia needs someone who understands her, who can guide her into the future while honoring her past."

"Well then, sugar," St. EOM said with a sly grin, "let's see what the leaves have to say about that, shall we?"

Now, my darlings, you must understand that reading tea leaves is as much an art as it is a science. And our St. EOM, bless his eccentric heart, was an artist in every sense of the word.

As Jimmy and Rosalynn finished their tea, St. EOM leaned forward, his eyes gleaming with a mix of mischief and otherworldly knowledge. "Alright, children," he said, though Jimmy was barely a decade his junior, "let's see what fate has in store for y'all."

He took Jimmy's cup first, swirling it three times counterclockwise—a habit he'd picked up from a Romani fortune teller in the East Village. As he peered into the cup, his expression changed, morphing from playful to serious in the blink of an eye.

"Well, Mr. Carter," he began, his voice low and gravelly, "I see a path rising before you. It's steep, mind you, and fraught with challenges. But at the top..." He paused for dramatic effect, and I swear you could hear a pin drop in that incense-filled room. "At the top, I see a house. A very big house. White as the driven snow."

Rosalynn gasped as her hand flew to her mouth. Jimmy, ever the pragmatist, simply raised an eyebrow. "The governor's mansion?"

St. EOM cackled, a sound that sent shivers down the Carters' spines. "Oh honey, think bigger. Much bigger."

Like the heavy Georgia humidity, the implications hung in the air. Jimmy cleared his throat, clearly uncomfortable with the weight of the prediction. "Now, let's not get ahead of ourselves. I haven't even announced my candidacy for governor yet."

"The leaves don't lie, sugar," St. EOM said with a shrug. "But they don't always tell the whole truth either. It's all about interpretation."

He turned his attention to Rosalynn's cup, and his eyes widened. "My, my, Mrs. Carter. You've got quite the journey ahead of you too. I see a lot of travel. And people—crowds of them, hanging on your every word."

Rosalynn blushed, but there was a glint of excitement in her eyes. "Really? But I'm just a simple Georgia girl."

"Ain't nothing simple about you, darlin'," St. EOM drawled. "You've got fire in your soul and steel in your spine. You'll need both for what's coming."

As the reading concluded, a comfortable silence fell over the room. St. EOM leaned back in his chair, lighting up another of his special cigarettes. The sweet, pungent smoke curled around them, adding to the dreamlike atmosphere.

"Now," he said, fixing Jimmy with a penetrating stare, "the question is, what are you going to do with this information?"

Jimmy sat up straighter, his jaw set with determination. "I'm going to run for governor, just as I planned. And if the people of Georgia see fit to elect me, I'll serve them to the best of my ability."

St. EOM nodded approvingly. "And after that?"

A small smile played on Jimmy's lips. "Well, we'll cross that bridge when we come to it, won't we?"

As the Studebaker disappeared down the dusty road, St. EOM stood at the gates of Pasaquan, an enigmatic smile on his face. "Well," he mused to himself, "things are certainly about to get interesting around here."

As the dust settled from the Carters' departure, St.

EOM found himself alone once again in his technicolor dreamland. The cicadas resumed their endless song, a droning lullaby that seemed to whisper the secrets of the cosmos.

Days at Pasaquan had a rhythm all their own, as fluid and unpredictable as the swirling patterns that adorned every surface. St. EOM would rise with the sun, his dreams still clinging to him like morning dew. He'd make his way to the garden, where rows of vegetables grew alongside more... shall we say, unconventional plants.

"Mornin', babies," he'd croon to his prized marijuana plants, their leaves stretching towards the Georgia sun. "Y'all behave now. We've got company coming."

And company did come, my dears. All sorts, from wide-eyed college students to weathered farmers, each drawn by the siren song of St. EOM's particular brand of enlightenment. Some came for the drugs, some for the fortunes, but all left changed in some ineffable way.

One sweltering afternoon, a beat-up Volkswagen van pulled up, spilling out a group of long-haired youngsters with flowers in their hair and revolution in their eyes.

"Far out, man," one of them breathed, taking in the psychedelic wonderland before them. "It's like... it's like the inside of my head, you know?"

St. EOM chuckled, sounding like gravel in a tin can. "Oh, honey, if this is what the inside of your head looks like, you might want to ease up on the acid."

He welcomed them in, of course. Regardless of how misguided, St. EOM never turned away a seeker. As the day wore on, the air grew thick with smoke, and the sound of sitar music drifted from a battered record player.

"You've gotta tell us, man," one of the girls said, her pupils dilated and her words slurring slightly. "What's it all mean? All this..." She gestured vaguely at the totemic sculptures and mandala designs.

St. EOM leaned back, taking a long drag from his ever-present joint. "Meaning? Oh, sugar, it doesn't mean a damn thing. And that's the beauty of it."

The girl's face scrunched up in confusion, but St. EOM continued, his voice taking on the cadence of a preacher at the pulpit. "You see, all these fine folks in town, they're always looking for meaning. In their bibles, in their bank accounts, in the color of a man's skin. But here?" He swept his arm out, encompassing all of Pasaquan. "Here, we celebrate the meaninglessness of it all. The pure, unadulterated joy of existence."

The young visitors nodded sagely, though it was unclear how much they truly comprehended through their drug-induced haze. As night fell, they curled up like kittens on St. EOM's mismatched furniture, sleeping off their cosmic journey.

Days turned to weeks, weeks to months, and the seasons marched on. St. EOM continued to add to his creation, with each new mural and sculpture a testament to the visions that haunted his dreams. The town's attitude towards him softened somewhat, moving from outright hostility to a kind of bemused tolerance.

One crisp autumn morning, a sleek 65 Ford Thunderbird pulled up to Pasaquan's gates. Out stepped a man in an impeccable suit, his salt-and-pepper hair slicked back with precision.

"Eddie, darling!" he called out, his New York accent a stark contrast to the Southern drawls St. EOM had grown accustomed to.

St. EOM's eyes widened in recognition. "Well, I'll be

damned. If it isn't Richard Copeland himself. What brings you down to these parts, sugar?"

Richard sauntered up, taking in the riot of color and form around him. "I was in Atlanta for a gallery opening and thought I'd swing by. See what you've been up to all these years."

As they walked the grounds, Richard regaled St. EOM with tales of the New York art scene. Names were dropped like confetti – Warhol, Pollock, and de Kooning.

"You could be up there with them, Eddie," Richard said, his voice taking on a cajoling tone. "This place... it's incredible. Outsider art is all the rage now. We could make you a star."

For a moment, St. EOM allowed himself to be transported back to those heady New York days. The parties, the acclaim, and the endless parade of wealthy patrons. But then he looked around at Pasaquan, at the world he'd built with his own two hands.

"Thanks, honey," he said softly, "but I think I'll stay right where I am."

Richard shook his head in disbelief but didn't push the issue. As he prepared to leave, he pressed a business card into St. EOM's hand. "If you ever change your mind..."

St. EOM tucked the card away, knowing he'd never use it.

The years rolled on, and Pasaquan grew ever more elaborate. But as his creation flourished, St. EOM himself began to fade. The wild eyes that had once sparkled with mischief now held a haunted look. His movements, once fluid and purposeful, became erratic.

The visions that had once been his inspiration now torment him. He would wake up at night, screaming about

Pasaquoyans and their impending doom. The steady stream of visitors slowed to a trickle, then stopped altogether.

In the town of Buena Vista, whispers began to circulate. "Poor Eddie," they'd say, shaking their heads. "Always knew he'd come to no good end."

On a cold winter's night in 1986, St. EOM sat alone in the heart of his creation. The colorful walls that had once brought him such joy now seemed to close in around him. He could hear the Pasaquoyans whispering, calling him home.

With shaking hands, he penned a final note. He bequeathed Pasaquan to the Buena Vista Ladies Art Club. His last act of defiance was a final thumb of the nose to the town that had never understood him.

"Let's see what they make of this," he chuckled mirthlessly.

As dawn broke over Pasaquan, painting the fantastic landscape in shades of gold and rose, St. EOM took his final breath. He was found later that day, surrounded by his life's work, a peaceful expression on his face.

The news spread through Buena Vista like wildfire. The Ladies Art Club, upon hearing of their inheritance, were at a loss. What were they to do with this garish, incomprehensible place?

"Well," said Mildred Hawkins, president of the club, "I suppose we could paint over it all. Make it into a nice, proper garden club."

But as they stood at the gates of Pasaquan, taking in the full scope of St. EOM's vision, even these proper Southern ladies felt a twinge of something. Respect? Awe? Or perhaps it was just a hint of the madness that had driven Eddie Owens Martin to create this wonderland in the first place.

In the end, they couldn't bring themselves to change a

thing. Pasaquan stood as it always had, a technicolor testament to one man's vision, a thorn in the side of conformity.

And on quiet nights, if you listen closely, you might just hear the sound of St. EOM's gravelly laugh on the wind, still reveling in his final joke on the good people of Buena Vista.

This concludes our tale, my dears. A story of art and madness, of vision and despair. St. EOM may have left this world, but Pasaquan remains a fever dream made real in Georgia's heart. And isn't that, in the end, all that any of us can hope for? To leave behind something that says, "I was here, and I was gloriously, unapologetically myself."

Act 3. The Ponderance: The Isolated Dreamers

As the sun rose over the red Georgia clay, Eddie Owens Martin—better known as St. EOM—stepped out of his humble abode and into a world of his own making. Vibrant mandalas, towering totems, and undulating walls of psychedelic patterns greeted him, as they did every morning. This was Pasaquan, a seven-acre visionary art environment that seemed to have sprouted from another dimension.

Miles away, in another corner of rural Georgia, Reverend Howard Finster was already hard at work in his Paradise Garden. His hands, worn from years of tinkering and creating, moved deftly as he transformed discarded objects into divine messages. Bicycle parts, dolls' heads, and fragments of mirrors came together in a symphony of folk art spirituality.

These two men, separated by distance but united in their isolation and creative fervor, were unwittingly crafting a testament to the power of seclusion in art. Their stories, intertwined with the landscapes they sculpted, paint a compelling picture of what happens when an artist is left alone with their visions.

St. EOM's Pasaquan is a riot of color and form, blending influences from Native American, African, and pre-Columbian cultures into something entirely new. The geometric patterns that adorn every surface pulse with an energy that seems to defy the sleepy rural setting. Here, in this secluded patch of Georgia, Martin was free to explore the depths of his imagination, unencumbered by the art world's trends or society's expectations.

Finster's Paradise Garden, while born of a different vision, shares that sense of unbridled creativity. Biblical verses mingle with pop culture references, creating a uniquely American folk art tapestry. The World's Folk Art Church stands as a beacon of Finster's peculiar blend of religious fervor and artistic compulsion. In Paradise Garden, everyday objects are elevated to the status of holy relics, each piece telling a story that only Finster could conceive.

As we wander through these extraordinary environments, a question begins to form: Could such pure, unfiltered visions emerge in today's hyperconnected world?

Imagine, for a moment, St. EOM with an Instagram account or Reverend Finster with a TikTok following. Would the pressure to create content to gain likes and shares have altered their artistic journeys? Would the constant influx of images and ideas from around the globe have diluted their unique perspectives?

In our modern world, artists are more connected than ever before. They can see works from every corner of the globe, attend virtual gallery openings, and engage with audiences instantly at the touch of a screen. This connectivity brings undeniable benefits—exposure, inspiration, and community. But as we scroll through endless feeds of carefully curated art, a creeping sense of homogeneity begins to set in.

The algorithm favors certain styles, certain colors, and certain compositions. Suddenly, everyone's work starts to look a little bit the same. The rough edges are smoothed out, and the weird bits are polished away. In this landscape, would there be room for a Pasaquan or a Paradise Garden?

Moreover, in a world where an artwork's value is increasingly determined by its price tag or its number of likes, what happens to art that doesn't easily fit into these metrics? St. EOM and Reverend Finster created their environments out of a deep, personal necessity, not with an eye towards the art market or social media engagement.

As we stand at this crossroads of art and technology, of isolation and connectivity, we must ask ourselves: Are we losing something vital? Are we trading the raw, unfiltered visions of isolated dreamers for a more palatable, marketable form of creativity?

Perhaps the answer lies in finding a balance. We can embrace the benefits of our interconnected world while also creating space for isolation and introspection. Artist residencies in remote locations, digital detox retreats, or simply setting aside time to disconnect and create without the pressure of immediate sharing—these could be ways to recapture some of that isolated creative spirit.

We must also reconsider how we value art. Looking beyond market prices and social media metrics, we can appreciate works for their cultural significance, their innovative spirit, and their ability to challenge and move us. In doing so, we make room for the next St. EOM or Howard Finster—artists whose visions might not fit neatly into a square photo or a short video but who have the power to transform a patch of rural Georgia, or indeed, our understanding of what art can be.

As the sun sets on Pasaquan and Paradise Garden, casting long shadows across their fantastical landscapes, we're reminded of the power of creative isolation. In a world that's increasingly uniform, these places stand as monuments to individuality, to the strange and wonderful visions that can emerge when an artist is left alone with their dreams.

The legacy of St. EOM and Reverend Finster challenges us to create space for such visions in our modern world. It urges us to value the unique, the personal, the culturally specific—even, or especially, when it doesn't fit neatly into our interconnected, algorithm-driven culture. For it is in these isolated dreamscapes that we often find the truest reflections of our diverse, complex, and endlessly creative human spirit in these isolated dreamscapes.

As we conclude our journey through the psychedelic wonderland of Pasaquan and the extraordinary life of St. EOM, we find ourselves at the intersection of art, spirituality, and the human quest for meaning. Like the swirling hues of a Purple Haze cocktail, the story of Eddie Owens Martin blends the vibrant colors of creativity, the intoxicating spirit of nonconformity, and the bittersweet notes of isolation into a complex, unforgettable concoction.

St. EOM's Pasaquan stands as a testament to the raw power of unfettered imagination. In this secluded corner of Georgia, far from the prying eyes of art critics and societal expectations, a visionary was free to paint his dreams across seven acres of red clay. The result is a kaleidoscopic fever dream made real, a place where mandalas pulse with cosmic energy and totemic figures stand sentinel over a world entirely of one man's making.

But Pasaquan is more than just an artistic achievement. It's a challenge to our modern, hyperconnected world. In an age where creativity is often measured in likes and shares, where algorithms shape our aesthetic preferences, and where the pressure to produce content is constant, St. EOM's isolated dreamscape reminds us of the value of disconnection. It poses the question: What visions might we realize if we allowed ourselves the space and time to dive deep into our own psyches, free from the noise of the outside world?

The tale of St. EOM also serves as a poignant reminder of the thin line between genius and madness. As his creation flourished, the man himself began to fade, haunted by visions that once inspired but are now tormented. It's a stark illustration of the price some artists pay for their gifts, a cautionary tale wrapped in a technicolor dream.

Yet, even in his final act, St. EOM's irreverent spirit shone through. By bequeathing Pasaquan to the Buena Vista Ladies Art Club, he delivered one last wink and nudge to the community that never quite understood him. In doing so, he ensured that his vision would endure, continuing to challenge and inspire long after he was gone.

As we raise our Purple Haze cocktails in a toast to St. EOM, we're not just celebrating one man's artistic legacy. We're honoring the spirit of creative rebellion, the courage to be unapologetically one's self, and the power of art to transform not just a patch of Georgia clay, but our understanding of what's possible when imagination is given free rein.

In a world that often seems to value conformity and marketability, places like Pasaquan remind us of the importance of preserving spaces for the weird, the wonderful, and the wholly unique. They challenge us to look beyond the algorithm, to seek out and celebrate those visionaries who dance to the beat of their own cosmic drum.

So here's to St. EOM, to Pasaquan, and to all the isolated dreamers who dare to paint their visions large across the canvas of the world. May their creations continue to inspire us, challenge us, and remind us that sometimes the most profound truths are found not in the mainstream but in the beautiful, bewildering fringes of human creativity.

As the sun sets on Pasaquan, painting its fantastic land-scape in shades of purple and gold, we're left with a simple yet powerful truth: In a world that often feels increasingly homogenized, there will always be a place for those who dare to dream in technicolor. And as long as places like Pasaquan exist, there will always be a haven for those seeking to lose themselves in the wild, wonderful visions of unfettered imagination.

In the end, isn't that what we all seek? A place, whether physical or metaphorical, where we can be "gloriously, unapologetically ourselves"? St. EOM found his. Perhaps, inspired by his story, we could find ours too.

4

GIN AND SHADOWS

Act 1. The Spirits: Gin and Tonic

In the sultry heat of a Savannah summer, few things are as refreshing as a perfectly crafted gin and tonic. This classic cocktail, with its crisp bite and aromatic bouquet, sets the stage for our tale of mystery and intrigue centered around the Johnson Family Funeral Home. As we delve into the story, imagine yourself on a wrought-iron balcony overlooking the moss-draped streets, a cool glass in hand, bearing witness to the strange events unfolding in the historic district.

As twilight settles in, you feel the urge for something crisp and refreshing. The answer materializes in your mind: a perfectly crafted gin and tonic.

You begin by selecting a large, balloon-shaped glass from your cabinet. Its wide bowl promises to capture and enhance the drink's aromatic bouquet. You fill it generously with crystal-clear ice cubes; their gentle clinks are a prelude to the experience ahead.

Next, you reach for your prized bottle of gin. Perhaps it's

a classic London Dry, or maybe a more botanical-forward craft gin. The choice is yours, and it's part of what makes this drink so personal. You measure out a double shot, watching as the clear spirit gracefully cascades over the ice.

Now comes the moment of anticipation. You crack open a fresh bottle of tonic water, its effervescence audibly escaping as you twist off the cap. Slowly and deliberately, you pour the tonic down the side of the glass. As it meets the gin, it froths and bubbles, creating a misty, swirling dance within the glass.

Aim for a ratio of one part gin to three parts tonic, adjusting for your personal preference. As the liquid levels rise, so does your excitement.

But you're not quite finished. You reach for a plump, ripe lime. With a sharp knife, you cut a wheel, its green flesh a stark contrast to the pale cocktail. You run the lime around the glass rim before gently dropping it into the drink, releasing a burst of citrus oil across the surface.

For a final flourish, you decide to add a surprise element —perhaps a few juniper berries or a sprig of fresh rosemary. This extra touch will complement the gin's botanicals and elevate the entire experience.

You step back and admire your creation. The gin and tonic stand tall and proud, bubbles racing to the surface and carrying with them the complex aromas of juniper, citrus, and herbs. Condensation begins to form on the outside of the glass, promising a cool, invigorating sip.

As you lift the drink, the aroma hits you first—a perfect balance of botanical gin, bitter tonic, and zesty lime. You take a sip, and the flavors explode across your palate. The gin's warmth is tempered by the tonic's quinine bite, while the lime adds a perfect citrus note.

In this moment, you realize you've created more than

just a drink. This gin and tonic is a sensory journey—a perfect balance of flavors and textures. It's a reminder that sometimes, the simplest combinations can yield the most extraordinary results. As you settle into your favorite chair, drink in hand, you know that this is exactly how a summer evening should be spent.

Now, with your drink in hand, let's turn our attention to a different kind of spirit - the ghostly secrets of Savannah's past and the curious case of the Johnson Family Funeral Home. This tale goes back to Savannah, Georgia, where I spent some time in my younger days. I used to paint old houses there, and when I wasn't working, I'd often find myself on a friend's porch, sipping gin and tonics as the evening settled in.

One particular night has stuck with me all these years. My buddy and I were out on his third-floor balcony, enjoying our drinks and the warm Savannah night. That's when we saw something odd happening at the old funeral home down the street.

Now, I've turned this memory over in my mind countless times since then. The details have probably shifted a bit, colored by time and imagination. But the core of it - what we thought we saw that night - has become the seed of a story I've been cultivating for years.

It's funny how these moments stick with us, isn't it? A single, strange occurrence can spark our imagination and grow into something more. So let's dive into this tale - not as it exactly happened, because memory's a tricky thing, but as it's evolved in my mind over the years.

Pour yourself a drink if you like - gin and tonic optional - and let's explore this little piece of Savannah mystery together...

Act 2. The Tale: Gin and Tonic

Savannah, Georgia, and a gin and tonic.
  The two are just synonymous in my mind.
  The taste of the bitter tonic as its effervescence
  mixes with tinges of juniper over the tongue,
  and the taste of lime breaking over that ice-cold first sip.
  It is a drink that propels its bitter-draped intoxication
  by slowly sipping the spirit of Savannah's Spanish moss-
draped antebellum streets.

The ice clinked in my glass as I took another sip of gin and tonic, savoring the crisp bite that cut through the humid Savannah night. Kevin and I sat on his third-floor balcony, the ornate white columns of his latest renovation project framing our view of the street below. The soft glow of the streetlights cast long shadows, giving an ethereal quality to the Spanish moss that draped the live oaks like ghostly curtains.

"I'm telling you, man," Kevin said, running a hand through his disheveled hair, "this house is going to be the death of me. Every time I think I've fixed one thing, three more problems pop up."

I chuckled, shaking my head. "That's what you get for taking on a hundred-year-old mansion. What possessed you to leave your cushy New York apartment for this?"

Kevin gestured expansively with his drink, nearly sloshing it over the side. "I think INSANITY at this point ! " He deflated slightly, slumping in his chair. "And maybe a little bit of a midlife crisis."

I was about to respond when a flicker of movement caught my eye. Across the street, at the old Beaux-Arts-style mansion that housed the Johnson Family Funeral Home, a basement window was sliding open.

"Hey," I said, nudging Kevin. "Check that out."

We watched in fascinated silence as a figure emerged from the window, struggling with... was that a casket? A second figure appeared, helping to maneuver the long box out onto the overgrown lawn.

"What the hell?" Kevin whispered, leaning forward for a better look.

As our eyes adjusted to the darkness, we could make out more details. The two figures, appearing to be men, wore dark clothing.They worked quickly and efficiently, carrying the casket to a flatbed trailer that was parked just out of sight around the corner of the building.

"Should we... call someone?" I inquired, not taking my eyes off the scene.

Kevin shook his head. "And say what? 'Hello, police? We're watching some guys move a coffin in the middle of the night'? For all we know, this could be totally normal funeral home business."

But as we continued to watch, it became clear that this was far from normal. Over the next hour, we saw no fewer than six caskets removed from the basement and loaded onto the trailer. The men worked in near-silence, their movements precise and practiced.

Finally, the trailer was full. The two men exchanged a few quiet words, then one of them climbed into the cab of the truck while the other disappeared back into the basement window. The engine started with a low rumble, and the truck pulled away, vanishing into the night.

Kevin and I sat in stunned silence for a long moment, our drinks forgotten.

"Okay," I said finally. "That was weird, right? That wasn't just me?"

Kevin nodded slowly. "Definitely weird. But what do we do about it?"

I shrugged, suddenly feeling very sober. "I guess we wait and see what happens next."

We didn't have to wait long. The very next afternoon, as I was walking home from the old house I was painting on Bull Street, I noticed a commotion outside the Johnson Family Funeral Home. A group of official-looking people in suits gathered on the front steps, while a locksmith worked on the front door.

I slowed my pace, trying to look casual as I strained to overhear their conversation.

"...unpaid taxes going back five years," one of the suits was saying. "The state has no choice but to seize the property."

My eyebrows shot up. I quickened my step, eager to share this new development with Kevin.

When I arrived at his place, I found him elbow-deep in plaster dust, wrestling with some ancient wiring.

"You're not going to believe this," I said, relaying what I'd overheard.

Kevin sat back on his heels, a thoughtful expression on his face. "So that's what last night was about. They must have known the state was coming for them, so they were trying to salvage what they could."

"But why the caskets?" I wondered. "Surely those belong to... well, to the occupants."

Kevin shrugged. "Maybe they were empty display models? Or maybe..." He trailed off with a mischievous glint in his eye.

I groaned. "Oh no. I know that look. What are you planning?"

"Nothing illegal," he assured me. "I just think we should

take a closer look at our neighborhood funeral home. For historical preservation purposes, of course."

I knew I should say no. I knew we should leave well enough alone. But curiosity got the better of me. "Alright," I sighed. "What did you have in mind?"

A week later, we found ourselves standing on the steps of the Johnson Family Funeral Home, trying our best to look like serious potential buyers. Kevin had somehow managed to arrange a tour with the state officers responsible for the property seizure.

"Now, gentlemen," the officer said as he unlocked the front door, "I should warn you that the property is in a state of... disarray. The previous owners left in quite a hurry."

As we stepped inside, I had to stifle a gasp. The grand entryway, with its soaring ceilings and ornate moldings, spoke of a bygone era of elegance. An air of neglect marred the beauty, with dust covering every surface and a faint smell of decay lingering in the air. "The Johnson family lived on the second floor," our guide explained, leading us up a creaking staircase. "The main floor was used for viewings and services, while the basement housed the... preparation area."

I exchanged a glance with Kevin, both of us thinking of the midnight casket removal we'd witnessed.

The family's living quarters were a strange mix of normal domesticity and the trappings of their morbid profession. Family photos shared shelf space with urns and memorial plaques. A child's backpack lay abandoned in a corner, a stark reminder of the lives upended by the business closure.

"And up here," the officer said, leading us to a narrow staircase, "is the third floor. It hasn't been used in years, as far as we can tell."

The moment we stepped onto the third floor, I felt a chill run down my spine. Broken windows allowed pigeons to roost in the rafters, their soft coos echoing through the empty rooms. This must have been the servants' quarters once upon a time, but now it was a playground for shadows and dust.

"Charming," Kevin muttered, his eyes gleaming with the prospect of renovation.

As we made our way back down, the officer hesitated outside a closed door on the main floor. "This is the embalming room," he said. "It's... well, it's a bit unsettling. Are you sure you want to see it?"

We nodded, steeling ourselves for whatever gruesome sight awaited us.

The room was clinically white, a stark contrast to the warm woods and rich colors of the rest of the house. At its center stood a stainless steel table, surrounded by an array of instruments I didn't want to examine too closely.

But it was the details that truly unnerved me. A child's dress hung from a hook on the wall, its cheerful floral pattern incongruous in this sterile setting. Makeup sponges were scattered across a nearby counter, with some still stained with the pigments used to give the dead the illusion of life.

"It looks like they left in a hurry," Kevin observed, his voice unnaturally loud in the quiet room.

The officer nodded. "When we came to serve the seizure notice, the place was empty. No sign of the family, just... this." He gestured around the room.

As we left the embalming room, I couldn't shake the feeling that we were missing something important. The midnight casket removal, the hasty departure of the

Johnson family, the eerie abandoned quality of the house—it all added up to... what?

Back out on the street, Kevin and I stood in silence for a moment, processing what we'd seen.

"So," Kevin said finally, "still want to go halves on a haunted funeral home?"

I snorted. "I think I'll pass, thanks. But seriously, what do you make of all this?"

Kevin shrugged. "Best case scenario? The family knew they were about to lose everything, so they tried to salvage what they could. Worst case..." He trailed off, leaving the unspoken possibilities hanging in the air.

"You don't think they actually... I mean, with the bodies?" I couldn't bring myself to finish the thought.

"I don't know," Kevin said. "And honestly, I'm not sure I want to know. Some mysteries are better left unsolved."

As we walked back to Kevin's place, I found myself glancing over my shoulder at the looming silhouette of the funeral home. In the fading light, it seemed to watch us go; its darkened windows looked like unseeing eyes, guarding whatever secrets lay within its walls.

That night, as I lay in bed, I couldn't shake the image of that child's dress hanging in the embalming room. Whom had it belonged to? Why was it there? And where is its owner now?

Sleep was a long time coming, and when it did, my dreams were filled with shadowy figures moving caskets in the night, their contents a mystery I both longed for and feared unraveling.

The next morning, over coffee at the local diner, Kevin and I tried to piece together what we knew.

"Okay," I said, ticking off points on my fingers. "We've got a funeral home that hasn't paid taxes in years. We've got a midnight moving operation. We've got a family that vanished into thin air. And we've got a creepy abandoned mansion full of... well, creepy abandoned funeral stuff."

Kevin nodded, stirring his coffee absently. "Don't forget the pigeons. Very important to the ambiance."

I rolled my eyes. "Focus, please. What are we missing?"

"Maybe nothing," Kevin said with a shrug. "Maybe it's exactly what it looks like - a family business gone under, trying to salvage what they could before the state took everything."

"But the caskets," I pressed. "Why move those in the middle of the night?"

Kevin leaned back in his chair, a thoughtful expression on his face. "Well, think about it. If you're a funeral home going out of business, what's your most valuable asset?"

I blinked. "The... caskets?"

"Bingo," Kevin said, pointing at me. "Now, I'm not saying they did anything illegal. But if they had pre-paid customers, people who had already bought plots or services... well, they might feel obligated to fulfill those contracts, even if it meant moving the, uh, clients."

It made a certain kind of sense, but something still nags at me. "But where would they take them? And why not just explain the situation to the families?"

Kevin spread his hands. "Pride? Shame? Maybe they thought they could still somehow save the business. Or maybe..." He trailed off, his eyes widening slightly.

"What?" I prompted.

"Maybe they were trying to protect someone," he said slowly. "Think about it - a family-run business, generations of history in that house. What if there was something in those records, or... or in those caskets, that they couldn't let the state find?"

The idea sent a chill down my spine. "You think they were hiding something?"

Kevin shrugged. "It's just a theory. But it would explain the secrecy, the midnight move, the hasty disappearance."

We sat in silence for a moment, the weight of the possibilities hanging between us.

"So what do we do now?" I asked finally.

Kevin drained the last of his coffee. "Nothing," he said firmly. "We're not detectives, and we're certainly not equipped to handle whatever might be going on here. We keep our heads down, we mind our own business, and we let the proper authorities handle it."

I nodded, relieved. As curious as I was, the thought of digging deeper into this mystery filled me with a nameless dread.

As we left the diner, I couldn't help but glance down the street toward the funeral home. In the bright morning light, it looked almost normal—just another grand old house in a city full of them. But now I knew the secrets that lurked behind its facade, the questions that haunted its empty rooms.

Kevin clapped me on the shoulder. "Come on," he said. "I've got a house full of century-old wiring to replace. Want to lend a hand?"

I laughed, grateful for the distraction. "Sure, why not? It's got to be less creepy than embalming rooms and midnight casket movers."

As we walked back to Kevin's renovation project, I tried to put the Johnson Family Funeral Home out of my mind. But I couldn't shake the feeling that this wasn't the end of the story. In a city as old as Savannah, with its layers of history and fondness for ghosts, some mysteries have a way of refusing to stay buried.

Weeks passed, and life in our little corner of Savannah settled back into its usual rhythms. Kevin continued his Sisyphean battle with his renovation project, and I threw myself into my work scraping and painting houses. The Johnson Family Funeral Home stood silent and empty, a "For Sale by Auction" sign swinging gently in the breeze.

But every now and then, usually late at night when the city was quiet and the moss-draped trees cast strange shadows, I'd find myself drawn to my window, staring across at the darkened mansion. Sometimes, I could have sworn I saw movement behind those dusty windows—a flicker of light, a shifting shadow. However, it was probably just my imagination, fueled by too many ghost stories and too much late-night gin.

On one such night, as I was about to turn away from the window and force myself to get some sleep, I saw it. A car moving slowly down the street with its headlights off. It pulled up in front of the funeral home and sat idling for a long moment.

My heart began to race. Was this connected to the midnight casket movers? Had the Johnson family returned?

I was just reaching for my phone to call Kevin when two figures emerged from the car. Even in the dim light, I could make out the suits and official-looking badges. Whatever this was, it wasn't clandestine - it was official.

I watched as the figures disappeared around the side of the house, presumably heading for the basement entrance we'd seen used that fateful night. For nearly an hour, I stood at my window, barely breathing, waiting to see what would happen next.

Finally, the figures reappeared. They were carrying something between them—not a casket this time, but what looked like boxes of files. They loaded these into the trunk of their car, had a brief conversation, then drove away as quietly as they'd come.

The next morning, I was at Kevin's door before he'd even had his first cup of coffee.

"Whoa, slow down," he said as I rattled off what I'd seen. "You're saying the feds, or whoever, were poking around the funeral home in the middle of the night?"

I nodded empathically. "It has to be connected to whatever the Johnson family was up to, right? Maybe they found something when they were inventorying the property for the auction."

Kevin rubbed his chin thoughtfully. "Could be. Or it could be totally unrelated. Maybe they just didn't want to draw attention to whatever they were doing."

"But what were they doing?" I pressed. "And why all the secrecy?"

Kevin shrugged. "Your guess is as good as mine. But I still think we should stay out of it. Whatever's going on, it's clearly above our pay grade."

I knew he was right, but I couldn't shake the feeling that we were somehow involved now, whether we wanted to be or not.

As the days wore on, more strange occurrences piled up. The funeral home had unmarked vans parked outside at odd hours. Men in hazmat suits enter and leave the basement. And through it all, there was no word from the Johnson family or any official explanation.

The neighborhood started to talk. Theories ranged from the mundane (toxic mold remediation) to the outlandish (secret government experiments). But no one seemed to know the truth.

It all came to a head one sweltering afternoon in late August. Kevin and I were on his balcony again, seeking refuge from the heat in the shade of the columns as well as the cool of our gin and tonics. We'd been discussing his latest renovation woes when a commotion across the street caught our attention.

A group of people had gathered in front of the funeral home. As we watched, more cars arrived, disgorging serious-looking men and women in suits. News vans began to pull up, reporters jockeying for position.

"What the hell?" Kevin muttered, leaning forward for a better look.

Before I could respond, a hush fell over the crowd. A man in a crisp suit had stepped up to a hastily assembled podium on the funeral home's front steps. Cameras flashed as he cleared his throat and began to speak.

Even from our perch across the street, we could hear his words clearly in the still afternoon air.

"Good afternoon. I'm Special Agent Thompson with the FBI. We're here today to announce the conclusion of a multi-year investigation into a complex financial fraud scheme..."

Kevin and I exchanged wide-eyed glances as the agent continued.

The Johnson Family Funeral Home, under the guise of legitimate business operations, was in fact the center of a vast money laundering operation. We have evidence of connections to organized crime syndicate

The auction day was approaching, and the state had decided to offer one final tour for potential buyers. Kevin, ever the opportunist, had managed to get us on the list. As we approached the imposing facade of the Johnson Family Funeral Home, I couldn't shake the feeling that we were about to step into something we shouldn't.

"Remember," Kevin muttered as we climbed the front

steps, "we're just interested buyers. No need to mention anything about midnight casket movers or mysterious government agents."

I nodded, trying to look nonchalant as we joined the small group gathered in the foyer. Our guide, a harried-looking woman from the state's asset seizure department, cleared her throat to get everyone's attention.

"Good morning, everyone. I'm Claire, and I'll be showing you around the property today. As you know, this building is being auctioned as-is, so please keep in mind that any renovations or repairs will be the responsibility of the buyer."

As we moved from room to room, I found myself hanging back, taking in details I'd missed on our first visit. The grand parlor, once a place of solemn gatherings, now felt hollow and abandoned. Dust motes danced in the shafts of sunlight that penetrated the heavy curtains, and the antique furniture stood like silent sentinels, waiting for families that would never return.

In the corner, a massive grandfather clock stood frozen at 3:15, its pendulum stilled. I wondered if that had been the moment the Johnsons realized their time was up and that their secrets were about to come crashing down around them.

We moved into what had once been the casket showroom. Empty platforms lined the walls; their rich velvet coverings now faded and moth-eaten. A few neglected floral arrangements, whose silk flowers were dusty and bedraggled, added to the air of decay.

"Man," Kevin whispered, "imagine trying to sell someone a casket in here. Talk about a tough pitch."

I shot him a look, but I had to admit, the room did have a certain morbid humor to it now. It was as if we were witnessing the funeral of the funeral home itself.

As we climbed the stairs to the second floor, I noticed something I'd overlooked before. Intricate carvings adorned the banister, featuring tiny, macabre scenes instead of the floral motifs you might expect.macabre scenes. Skeletons danced as the living, grinning skull faces peered out from leafy branches. It was beautiful in its own way, but undeniably creepy.

The family's living quarters were much as we'd seen them before, frozen in time like some bizarre museum exhibit. But this time, I noticed a door we hadn't explored on our previous visit.

"What's through there?" I asked Claire, pointing to the closed door.

She consulted her clipboard. "That would be... ah, yes. The children's room. We can take a quick look, but please don't touch anything."

As the door swung open, a wave of sadness washed over me. Two small beds stood against opposite walls, their cheerful quilts a stark contrast to the somber business conducted downstairs. A half-finished puzzle rested on a small table, while a teddy bear slumped in a rocking chair. It was as if the children had just stepped out for a moment, expecting to return any minute to resume their play.

"Did they have much warning?" one of the other potential buyers asked. "Before the seizure, I mean."

Claire shook her head. "From what we understand, it all happened quite suddenly. The family left with little more than the clothes on their backs."

I thought of the midnight casket movers and their hasty departure. How much had the children known? Had they understood what was happening, or had they simply been whisked away in the night, leaving behind the only home they'd ever known?

As we made our way back downstairs, Kevin nudged me. "Check it out," nodding towards a small office off the main hallway.

I peered in, not sure what I was looking for at first. Then I saw it. The desk calendar was still open for the month the Johnsons had left. Most of the days were filled with normal funeral home business—viewings, services, and consultations. But there, on the 15th, was a single word scrawled in red ink: "DEADLINE."

Before I could point it out to Kevin, Claire was ushering us along. "Now, if you'll follow me, we'll take a look at the basement area."

The temperature seemed to drop several degrees as we descended the narrow stairs. The walls down here were bare cinderblock, a stark contrast to the ornate decor above. Pipes ran along the ceiling, their gentle creaking the only sound in the oppressive silence.

"This is where most of the... preparation work was done," Claire explained, her voice echoing slightly in the confined space. "The embalming room is through here."

As we entered the room, I heard several sharp intakes of breath from our group. The clinical whiteness of the walls and floors seemed to glow in the dim light, making the stainless steel equipment stand out in sharp relief. Despite obvious attempts at cleaning, the embalming table dominated the center of the room, and its drain was still faintly stained. But it was the little details that truly brought home the nature of the work done here. A rack of chemicals with ominous warning labels. The shelf of makeup features muted tones, designed to mimic life in death rather than the cheerful colors of the living. And there, hanging from a hook, was the child's dress we'd seen before, its cheerful pattern now seeming more like a cruel joke.

"Jesus," Kevin muttered under his breath. "And I thought my house had bad vibes."

As Claire continued her spiel about the "excellent drainage system" and "state-of-the-art ventilation," I found my attention drawn to a corner of the room. There, partially hidden behind a supply cabinet, was a door I hadn't noticed on our previous visit.

"Excuse me," I said, interrupting Claire mid-sentence. "Where does that door lead?"

She blinked while following my gaze. "Oh, that? That's just a storage closet. Nothing interesting in there."

But something in her tone made me suspicious. As the group moved on to examine the "spacious refrigeration unit," I lingered behind. Glancing over my shoulder to make sure no one was watching, I quickly crossed to the door and tried the handle.

Locked.

"Hey," Kevin hissed from the doorway. "What are you doing? Come on, we're heading back upstairs."

I rejoined the group, my mind racing. Why would a simple storage closet be locked when the rest of the building was open for viewing? And why had Claire seemed so dismissive of it?

As we climbed back to the main floor, I hung back to walk beside Kevin. "Did you notice that locked door in the embalming room?" I whispered.

He nodded. "Yeah, weird, right? But maybe it's just where they kept the really valuable stuff. You know, gold fillings and whatnot."

I shot him a look. "That's not funny."

He shrugged. "Just trying to lighten the mood. This place gives me the creeps."

Back in the foyer, Claire wrapped up the tour with some

final notes about the auction process. As the group began to disperse, I noticed her slip a key from her pocket and hand it to a man I hadn't seen before - tall, with a close-cropped grey beard and the bearing of someone used to giving orders.

They exchanged a few quiet words, then the man nodded and headed towards the basement stairs.

"Come on," I said, tugging on Kevin's sleeve. "Let's get out of here."

As we stepped out into the bright Savannah sunshine, I felt as if I'd been holding my breath the entire time we were inside. The weight of the funeral home's secrets - both known and unknown - seemed to press down on me.

"Well," Kevin said, stretching his arms above his head, "that was... something. Still want to go halves on a haunted money-laundering funeral parlor?"

I managed a weak laugh. "I think I'll pass, thanks. But Kevin..."

"Yeah?"

"Did you notice that man at the end? The one Claire gave the key to?"

Kevin nodded slowly. "Yeah, I saw him. Looked like a fed to me. Why?"

I hesitated, not sure how to put my suspicions into words. "I just... I have a feeling we haven't heard the last of this place's secrets."

Kevin slung an arm around my shoulders as we walked back towards his house. "Maybe not. But whatever's going on, it's way above our pay grade. Let's leave the mystery-solving to the professionals, okay?"

I nodded, but I couldn't shake the feeling that somehow, someway, we were already too involved to simply walk away. As we crossed the street, I glanced back at the Johnson

Family Funeral Home. In the bright afternoon sun, it looked almost normal—just another grand old Savannah mansion with a story to tell.

Act 3. The Ponderance: Fading Mystery of Urban Spaces

In the heart of Savannah, Georgia, where Spanish moss drapes over centuries-old oaks, I met an old character of the city long ago. He owned an old Victorian mansion and was at all the social events about town. Alvin Neely was one of those genuine longtime citizens who had seen much in the way of change. He agreed to help me with my thesis project, which was a documentary about the gentrification of the city. Now, time has passed, and Alvin, like so many others I interviewed, has long since passed away.

Alvin Neely's words echo through time: "I kinda miss Savannah when it was dark and mysterious." This simple statement, captured during my graduate thesis work on gentrification, unlocked a profound understanding of urban transformation that has haunted me ever since.

What exactly is this "dark and mysterious" quality that Alvin, and so many others, yearn for in their changing neighborhoods? It's not just about dimly lit streets or the thrill of the unknown. It's a complex tapestry of authenticity, cultural vibrancy, and the raw energy of spaces yet untamed by the homogenizing forces of development.

I've witnessed this myself, in fleeting moments that seem to capture the essence of a place on the cusp of change. I saw empty caskets being "stolen back" from the funeral home seized by the state. That scene was surreal, reminiscent of the dark and mysterious moments prevalent in Savannah at that time. It was reminiscent of *Midnight in the*

Garden of Good and Evil, which had made the city infamous years before.

This spectrum of "dark and mysterious" isn't unique to Savannah. In Washington, D.C., I watched as beloved neighborhood bars – havens of friendship and community – slowly disappeared, priced out by rising rents and changing tastes. Each closure felt like a small death, marking the loss of a space where people forged real connections over cheap beers and shared stories.

What happens when the soul of a neighborhood is slowly squeezed out? It's not just about buildings or businesses; it's about the people who gave those spaces life. What happens to the poets, the musicians, and the eccentric characters who made these places vibrant when they can no longer afford to live there?

People often portray gentrification as progress—a revitalization of neglected areas. But in this process, we risk sanitizing away the very things that make these neighborhoods special. The gritty authenticity, the sense of possibility, the feeling that anything could happen – these are the qualities that draw people to urban spaces in the first place.

Yet, it's crucial to recognize that nostalgia can often gloss over real issues. The "dark and mysterious" past wasn't always romantic. It often went hand in hand with poverty, crime, and neglect. The challenge we face is how to improve living conditions and opportunities for residents without erasing the cultural fabric that makes a place unique.

As our cities continue to evolve, we're seeing a growing awareness of what's at stake. Community land trusts, rent control measures, and efforts to preserve cultural institutions are all attempts to strike a balance between development and preservation. But are these enough to maintain the soul of a place?

Perhaps the most poignant aspect of this transformation is its inevitability. Like a tide slowly rising, gentrification reshapes our urban landscapes, leaving us to grapple with questions of identity, community, and belonging. As we move forward, we must ask ourselves: How can we honor the "dark and mysterious" history of our neighborhoods while building a future that's inclusive and vibrant for all?

In the end, the loss of these spaces is about more than just aesthetics or nostalgia. It's about the erasure of stories, the displacement of communities, and the homogenization of our urban experience. As we continue to develop our cities, we must strive to preserve the essence of what makes each place unique – that ineffable quality that Alvin Neely and so many others miss when it's gone.

As the sun sets on another day in Savannah, casting long shadows through the Spanish moss, I can't help but reflect on Alvin Neely's words and the changes I've witnessed in cities across America. The "dark and mysterious" quality he missed is more than just an atmosphere—it's the beating heart of a city's identity, the raw material from which its stories are woven. As we navigate the inevitable tides of progress and development, our challenge is not to halt change, but to shape it in a way that honors the past while building a future that's vibrant, inclusive, and authentically rooted in place. Perhaps the true art of urban evolution lies not in erasing the shadows but in learning to dance with them, preserving the magic and mystery that make our cities truly alive. In the end, it's not just about saving buildings or businesses, but about nurturing the soul of our communities—ensuring that the stories of yesterday can still whisper through the streets of tomorrow.

5

SOUTHERN DISCOMFORT

Act 1. The Spirits: Alabama Slammer

As the last sip of your Alabama Slammer slides down your throat, a warmth spreads through your chest, igniting a spark of adventure. The sweet, tangy flavors linger on your tongue, much like the promises of an untold story waiting to unfold. Little did you know that this cocktail, born from Southern charm and bold spirits, would be the prelude to a tale of friendship, resilience, and small-town intrigue. So settle into your seat, let the flavors of the South dance on your palate, and prepare to be transported to Pell City, Alabama, where a simple car breakdown is about to spiral into an unexpected journey.

As the sun dips low on a sultry Southern evening, you find yourself yearning for a taste of something bold and spirited. In a flash, the answer comes to you: the Alabama Slammer.

You begin by selecting a tall, sleek Collins glass from your collection. Its smooth surface catches the warm light of the setting sun, promising to showcase the vibrant hues of your creation.

First, you reach for the Southern Comfort, whose bottle is heavy with history and flavor. You pour a generous measure of the golden liquid pooling at the bottom of the glass. The sweet aroma of whiskey and fruit rises, setting the stage for what's to come.

Next comes the amaretto, whose nutty sweetness is a perfect complement to the Southern Comfort. As you pour, you can almost taste the almond notes on your tongue, anticipating how they'll meld with the other flavors.

Now for a burst of citrus. You grab a bottle of freshly squeezed orange juice from your fridge. The bright orange liquid splashes into the glass, its tartness cutting through the sweetness of the liqueurs.

But you're not done yet. You reach for the final key ingredient: sloe gin. Its deep ruby color is a stark contrast to the orange and gold already in your glass. When you pour, it creates beautiful swirls and eddies, like a sunset in a glass.

With all the ingredients assembled, you fill the glass with ice. The cubes clink against each other and the glass sides, creating a musical interlude in your cocktail creation.

Now comes the moment of truth. You cap your shaker over the glass and, with a fluid motion, begin to shake. The sounds of ice rattling and liquids mixing fill the air as you move with purpose, ensuring every element is perfectly combined.

After a vigorous shake, you pour the cocktail back into your Collins glass. The result is a stunning gradient of orange and red, reminiscent of an Alabama sunset.

For the finishing touch, slice an orange wheel and perch it on the glass rim. A maraschino cherry follows, slowly sinking through the layers of your creation. .

You step back to admire your handiwork. The Alabama Slammer stands before you, a testament to Southern charm and bold flavors. The glass frosts over slightly, promising a cool respite from the warm evening.

As you lift the glass to your lips, the fruity aroma hits you first. Then comes the taste—a perfect balance of sweet, tart, and spirit. It's complex yet approachable, much like the South itself.

In this moment, you realize you've captured more than just a cocktail. You've bottled a piece of Southern hospitality, a drink that tells a story with every sip. As you settle into your porch swing, Alabama Slammer in hand, you can't help but feel a connection to the rich tapestry of Southern cocktail culture. This, you think, is how a summer evening in Alabama should taste.

As you set your empty glass down, the essence of the Alabama Slammer still lingering in your senses, you can't help but draw parallels between this spirited concoction and the story about to unfold. Like the layers of flavors in your drink—the sweet whiskey, the tart citrus, and the nutty amaretto—the tale of Stacy and Mae promises to be a blend of friendship, adversity, and small-town dynamics. The Alabama Slammer may have quenched your thirst, but it has also whetted your appetite for adventure. So, with the taste of the South still on your lips, let's dive into the heart of Pell City, where our protagonists are about to discover that sometimes, life's most intriguing stories begin with an unexpected detour.

Picture this: A broken-down car, a repair shop parking lot, and a whole weekend stretched out before me in Pell City. Now, some might call that a recipe for boredom, but for a postmodern gypsy like myself, it was an opportunity for observation and inspiration.

As I watched the comings and goings of this small town, a story began to take shape in my mind. A story of two friends, a vintage Ford Ranger, and a small-town scam that would test their wits and resilience.

So grab your favorite road trip snack, settle in, and let me take you on a journey to Pell City, Alabama, where Stacy and Mae are about to discover that sometimes the real adventure begins when the wheels stop turning.

Act 2. The Story: Pell City

In the sweltering heart of Alabama, two friends uncover a sinister secret lurking beneath the surface of a sleepy small town. What begins as a simple reunion spirals into a high-stakes battle against a corrupt towing scheme that's been preying on unsuspecting visitors. Armed with nothing but their wits and a vintage Ford Ranger, Stacy and Mae find themselves caught in a web of small-town politics, hidden car lots, and a justice system that seems rigged against them. Can they expose the truth before more innocent people fall victim to the ultimate Southern inhospitality?

Stacy's vintage '70s Ford Ranger rumbled to a stop in the Walmart parking lot of Pell City, Alabama. The faded blue paint and rusted chrome bumper stood out among the sea of modern SUVs and minivans. Stacy, with her long auburn hair tied back in a messy bun and tattoos peeking out from under her flannel shirt, hopped out of the driver's seat.

She pulled out her phone and fired off a quick text to Mae: "Just got to Walmart. You still at the Hampton?"

A moment later, her phone buzzed with Mae's reply: "Yep! Room 203. Come on over!"

Stacy shouldered her well-worn canvas backpack and made her way across the street to the Hampton Inn. The automatic doors slid open with a whoosh, letting out a blast of air-conditioned air that was a welcome respite from the sticky Alabama heat.

As she rode the elevator up to the second floor, Stacy reflected on how surreal it felt to be out and about after months of sheltering in place due to the pandemic. She adjusted her cloth mask, decorated with little cartoon peaches—a nod to her organic produce business back in Decatur.

Mae answered the door with a squeal of excitement, pulling Stacy into a tight hug. "I can't believe we're actually doing this!" she exclaimed. "A real, in-person reunion!"

The two friends settled onto the crisp hotel bed, catching up on the past few months. Mae regaled Stacy with tales of teaching kindergarten virtually - "You wouldn't believe how hard it is to wrangle 5-year-olds over Zoom!" - while Stacy shared updates on her farmers market adventures.

As they chatted, Mae absently gazed out the window at the Walmart parking lot across the street. Suddenly, she sat bolt upright. "Wait a second... Stacy, isn't that your truck?"

Stacy leapt to the window, pressing her face against the glass. Indeed, a flatbed tow truck was lifting her beloved Ford Ranger onto its back.

"What the hell?!" Stacy exclaimed, already halfway out of the door. Mae scrambled to keep up as they raced down to the parking lot.

By the time they reached the truck, a small crowd had gathered. Stacy pushed her way through, waving her arms frantically. "Stop! That's my truck!"

The tow truck driver, a burly man with a handlebar mustache, barely glanced her way. "Sorry, missy. Just doin' my job."

"But I only parked there for like 20 minutes!" Stacy protested. "I was coming right back!"

A thin woman in a Walmart manager's smock sidled up, a toothless grin spreading across her face. "Well, well. Looks like we got ourselves a loiterer," she drawled, eyes raking over Stacy's tattoos and Mae's Agnes Scott College t-shirt. "You fancy educated types think you can just park wherever you want, huh?"

Stacy bristled. "I wasn't loitering, I was shopping!"

The manager's grin widened. "Oh yeah? Where's your receipt?"

As Stacy sputtered, trying to explain that she hadn't actually bought anything yet, she caught sight of the manager slipping a $100 bill into her bra. A sheriff's deputy lounging nearby winked at the manager.

"Listen here, little miss organic farmer," the manager sneered. "You want your truck back? That'll be $500 cash. Otherwise, it's off to the impound lot."

Stacy and Mae exchanged panicked looks. $500 cash? Where were they supposed to get that kind of money on a moment's notice?

As they debated their options, they overheard snippets of conversation from the crowd.

"...heard the sheriff's been doin' this for months..."

"...easy way to make a quick buck..."

"...bet that old truck would make a great huntin' vehicle..."

The realization dawned slowly but surely - this wasn't just a misunderstanding. This was a scam targeting unsuspecting out-of-towners.

For the next several hours, Stacy and Mae ran themselves ragged trying to get the truck back. They pleaded with the sheriff's office, only to be given the runaround.

They called every towing company in a 50-mile radius, but no one seemed to know where Stacy's truck had ended up.

As the sun began to set, the girls slumped onto a bench outside the Walmart, utterly defeated.

"What are we going to do?" With her head in her hands, Stacy moaned. "That truck is my livelihood. How am I supposed to run my business without it?"

Mae put a comforting arm around her friend's shoulders. "We'll figure something out. But right now, I don't think it's safe for us to stay here. Let's head to Birmingham for the night - we can regroup and come up with a plan in the morning."

An hour later, they found themselves settled into a room at the Hilton in downtown Birmingham. The sleek, modern decor was a far cry from the rundown Hampton Inn in Pell City.

"You know what we need?" Mae declared, a glint in her eye. "Drinks. Strong ones."

They made their way to a nearby bar in Five Points, sliding onto stools at the polished wooden counter. The bartender, a young woman with a purple mohawk, greeted them with a smile.

"What can I get for you ladies?"

Stacy and Mae exchanged looks. "Two Alabama Slammers," they said in unison.

As the bartender mixed their drinks, the opening synth riff of "Blinding Lights" by The Weeknd filled the air. The pulsing beat seemed to match their racing thoughts, a stark contrast to the laid-back atmosphere of the bar. Mae found herself tapping her foot to the rhythm, momentarily distracted from their troubles.

"I've been tryna call, I've been on my own for long enough," The Weeknd's voice crooned over the speakers.

Stacy couldn't help but draw a parallel to their current situation - they'd been trying to call for help, feeling isolated in this unfamiliar town. As the chorus hit, the bar's energy shifted, a few patrons moving to the beat, their worries temporarily forgotten in the music.

As they sipped their drinks - a potent concoction of Southern Comfort, amaretto, and orange juice - they recounted the day's events.

"I still can't believe it," Stacy said, shaking her head. "How can they just... take someone's car like that?"

Mae frowned thoughtfully. "It's like... they're taking advantage of this whole pandemic situation. People are desperate and scared. Easy targets."

Stacy nodded, twirling her straw in her glass. "And we're the outsiders. The 'fancy educated types,'" she added, mimicking the Walmart manager's sneering tone.

"Hey," Mae said suddenly, sitting up straight. "You know what? Screw them. We are fancy-educated types. And we're going to use that education to figure this out."

Stacy couldn't help but smile at her friend's determination. "You're right. Tomorrow, we'll hit the library, look up local laws. Maybe we can find a loophole or something."

As they clinked glasses, a sense of renewed purpose washed over them. They may have lost this battle, but the war was far from over.

The bartender overheard their conversation and leaned in. "Y'all havin' truck trouble in Pell City?" She sympathetically shook her head at their nods. "Ain't the first time I've heard that story. Lemme give you the number of my cousin - he's a lawyer, specializes in this kinda thing."

As Stacy jotted down the number, she felt a glimmer of hope. Maybe, just maybe, they'd be able to turn this Alabama Slammer around.

The week that followed was a blur of frustration and anxiety for Stacy. She'd returned to Atlanta, her plans for a relaxing lake weekend with friends completely derailed. Every day, she called the tow company, only to be met with vague promises and noncommittal answers.

"We'll call you when we have an update, ma'am," the bored-sounding receptionist would drawl, clearly uninterested in Stacy's plight.

In between calls, Stacy scoured the internet for information about Pell City's towing practices. What she found made her blood run cold.

One night, as she sat cross-legged on her shabby-chic couch, scrolling through yet another online forum, she stumbled upon a post that made her gasp.

"Y'all won't believe this," the post began. "Pell City's got this crazy loophole law. They can auction off 'abandoned' vehicles after just a week. And guess what? They get to decide what counts as 'abandoned.' Been hearing stories of folks losing their rides after parking in the wrong spot for just a few hours."

Stacy's fingers flew across her phone screen as she dialed Mae.

"Mae, you're not gonna believe this," she said as soon as her friend picked up. "They might be trying to auction off my truck!"

Mae's voice crackled through the speaker, thick with disbelief. "No way. That can't be legal!"

"Apparently, it is," Stacy sighed. "At least in Pell City."

As the days dragged on, Stacy heard more horror stories. A college student lost his car while visiting his grandmother. A single mom's minivan was towed while she was working a double shift at the diner. Each tale added to the knot of dread in Stacy's stomach.

Finally, on the sixth day, Stacy's phone rang. The caller ID showed an unfamiliar number with a Pell City area code.

"Ms. Johnson?" a gruff voice said when she answered. "This is Bubba from Big Al's Towing. We've located your vehicle."

Stacy's heart leapt. "Oh, thank God! Where is it? When can I come get it?"

"Well, now," Bubba drawled, "that's the thing. Seems your truck's been moved to one of our satellite lots. You'll need to come down here in person to sort out the paperwork."

Stacy's relief quickly turned to suspicion. "Satellite lots? Why was it moved?"

"Just company policy, ma'am," Bubba replied, his tone leaving no room for argument. "You coming or not?"

Stacy bit back a frustrated groan. "Fine. I'll be there tomorrow morning."

The next day, I found Stacy on a cramped shuttle from Atlanta to Birmingham, her leg bouncing with nervous energy. From Birmingham, she ordered an Uber to take her to the small town outside Pell City where Big Al's Towing was supposedly located.

The Uber driver, a chatty woman named Doreen, filled the ride with local gossip. As they drove, the soft strains of a country song drifted from the radio. Stacy recognized Tim McGraw's voice singing "I Called Mama."

"You heading to Big Al's?" Doreen inquired, slightly lowering the volume. "Lord, honey, good luck with that. That place is shadier than a magnolia tree in July."

Stacy's eyebrows shot up. "What do you mean?"

Doreen lowered her voice conspiratorially, the gentle guitar of the song underscoring her words. "Well, let's just say Big Al and the sheriff go way back. Lots of folks 'round here lost their cars to those two."

As they pulled into the small southern village, Stacy's unease grew. The town seemed almost too quaint, like a movie-set version of a sleepy Southern hamlet. But something felt off. The lyrics "Sometimes you've gotta call mama" seemed to take on a new meaning in light of her situation.

"This is as far as I go, honey," Doreen said, pulling up to a dusty crossroads. The song faded out as she turned off the engine. "Big Al's is just down that dirt road. You be careful now, ya hear?"

Stacy thanked her and set off down the road, her sneakers kicking up little clouds of red clay dust. As she walked, she began to notice something strange. Behind weathered fences and overgrown hedges, she caught glimpses of cars. Lots of cars.

Curiosity got the better of her, and she veered off the main road, following a barely-there path between two dilapidated barns. What she found made her jaw drop.

Hidden from view was a vast lot filled with vehicles of all kinds. Some were obviously old junkers, but others looked nearly new. A shiny red sports car sat next to a muddy pickup truck. A minivan with "Baby on Board" stickers was parked beside a motorcycle.

Stacy's mind raced. Were all of these "abandoned" vehicles? How many people have fallen victim to this scheme? The echo of Tim McGraw's song played in her head, and she felt a sudden, strong urge to call her own mama for advice.

She continued her exploration, finding more hidden lots scattered throughout the town. Each discovery added to her growing sense of outrage.

Finally, she arrived at Big Al's Towing, a run-down office

with a neon "OPEN" sign flickering in the window. Inside, she found Bubba, a portly man with a thick mustache and a sweat-stained shirt.

"'Bout time you showed up," he grunted. "Your truck's out back. Follow me."

He led her through a maze of junk cars to a far corner of the lot. Her beloved Ford Ranger was there, partially hidden under a tarp.

Stacy's relief at seeing her truck was quickly overshadowed by anger. "Why is it all the way out here? And what's with all these other cars?"

Bubba's eyes narrowed. "Now, don't you go stickin' your nose where it don't belong, missy. You want your truck or not?"

Swallowing her fury, Stacy nodded. "How much do I owe you?"

The amount Bubba quoted made her eyes water, but she handed over the cash, her hands shaking with suppressed rage.

As she climbed into her truck, Bubba called out, "Pleasure doing business with ya!" As she peeled out of the lot, his mocking laughter followed her.

The drive home was a blur of emotions - relief at having her truck back, anger at the injustice of it all, and a gnawing sense of guilt for those who weren't as fortunate as her.

As soon as she got home, Stacy pulled out her phone and dialed Mae.

"You are not going to believe what just happened," she said as soon as Mae picked up.

While she talked, Stacy rummaged through her kitchen, pulling out bottles at random. She needed a drink, and it needed to be strong.

"So there I was, in this creepy little town, surrounded by

hidden car lots," Stacy continued, pouring a generous amount of whiskey into a mason jar. "It was like some kind of automotive black market!"

She added a splash of sweet tea, a squeeze of lemon, and a handful of mint leaves she'd been growing on her windowsill.

"And get this," she said, taking a long swig of her concoction. "When I finally got to Big Al's, they had my truck hidden under a tarp in the back of the lot. Like they were trying to keep it out of sight or something."

Mae's gasp of outrage came through clearly. "That's insane! We've got to do something about this, Stacy. We can't let them keep getting away with it."

Stacy nodded, even though Mae couldn't see her. "You're right. This isn't just about my truck anymore. It's about all those other people who've lost their cars."

As she continued to recount her adventure, Stacy's mind was already whirring with possibilities. Maybe she could contact the lawyer mentioned by the bartender. Or contact a local news station. There had to be a way to expose this scam and bring it to an end.

Act 3. The Ponderance: The Quiet Erosion of Local Awareness

Picture this: You're driving through a small town, the kind of place where everybody knows everybody. The streets are lined with mom-and-pop shops, and there's a sense of community that feels almost tangible. But beneath this Norman Rockwell veneer, something sinister lurks. Welcome to the world of "Alabama Slammer," the latest episode of my podcast, Postmodern Gypsy.

Now, you might be thinking, "Corruption in a small

town? Surely we'd hear about that." And therein lies the rub, folks. We've become so accustomed to the noise of national headlines and Twitter feuds that we've lost our ear for the whispers in our own backyards.

Let me take you back to a time when I found myself as a fly on the wall in a community not unlike the one in our story. Pell City, Alabama, - a place where the air is thick with humidity and secrets. I heard tales of shady dealings that would make your hair stand on end. Under the noses of unsuspecting owners, cars disappear into a quasi-legal loophole of modern living. It's the kind of thing you'd think couldn't happen in broad daylight, but oh, it does.

But here's the kicker - it's not just about a few stolen cars. This willful blindness, this societal glazing over, it's everywhere. Think about it. How many times have you heard about entire water districts being advised not to drink from their taps due to contamination? Or what about that grove of century-old oaks, living witnesses to history, suddenly bulldozed for a golf course? Where was the outcry? Where were the picket signs and the angry mobs?

So, how did we get here? Well, it's a perfect storm, really. First off, we're drowning in information. Our phones are constantly pinging with alerts about what some celebrity had for breakfast or the latest political gaffe in Washington. Meanwhile, the story about local officials enriching themselves often lands on page six, if it even makes it into the paper. And speaking of papers, where have all the local ones gone? Remember when the town paper was as much a part of your morning routine as that first cup of coffee? Now, investigative journalism at the local level is going the way of the dodo. Without those watch dogs sniffing around, the foxes are having a field day in the henhouse.

But it's not just about the news we're getting - or not

getting. It's also about what we allow ourselves to believe. There's this mentality, this "it can't happen here" syndrome that's as American as apple pie. We like to think our town, our community, is somehow immune to the rot we see elsewhere. It's a comforting thought, sure, but it's also a dangerous one. Because while we're patting ourselves on the back for our supposed moral superiority, the bad actors are working overtime.

And let's not forget about the labyrinth of modern bureaucracy. These days, it takes a law degree and a magnifying glass to understand half of what goes on in local government. Is it any wonder that schemes like the one in "Alabama Slammer" can operate in plain sight? When the system is a Rube Goldberg machine of legal loopholes and red tape, it's all too easy for the unscrupulous to game it.

The real tragedy, though, is what happens when we let this go on for too long. Those ancient oaks I mentioned? They're gone now, replaced by perfectly manicured greens where the local bigwigs can work on their putts. That contaminated water? Well, let's just say I wouldn't be filling my canteen from those taps anytime soon. And with each scandal that goes unnoticed and each shady deal that slips through the cracks, we lose a little bit more of what makes our communities worth living in.

So what's the answer? How do we shake off this collective cataract and start seeing clearly again? Well, for starters, we need to tune back into our local frequencies. Support that scrappy local paper, even if it's just a guy with a blog and a burning desire for the truth. Show up to town hall meetings - and not just when they're talking about raising property taxes. Use those social media skills for more than just sharing cat videos; spread the word when something smells fishy in your neck of the woods.

So the next time you're driving through your town, take a good, hard look around. What don't you see? What aren't you hearing? Because in the silence, in the spaces between the official narratives and the glossy tourist brochures, that's where the real stories are waiting to be told.

And who knows? Maybe you'll be the one to tell them.

As the ice melts in your glass, diluting the last traces of your Alabama Slammer, you can't help but draw parallels between this cocktail and the story that's unfolded before you. Like the layers of the drink - the sweet Southern Comfort, the tart orange juice, and the complex amaretto - our tale of Stacy and Mae's misadventure in Pell City is a blend of flavors, each adding depth to the overall experience.

The Alabama Slammer, much like small-town America, presents an enticing facade. It's sweet, inviting, and steeped in tradition. But just as the potent spirits lurk beneath the fruity exterior of the drink, so too does corruption simmer under the surface of seemingly idyllic communities.

Stacy and Mae's journey began with a simple car breakdown - an inconvenience that spiraled into a confrontation with systemic corruption. Their story serves as a microcosm of a larger issue: the quiet erosion of local awareness and accountability.

As we've seen, this erosion isn't loud or dramatic. It's a slow, insidious process, much like the gradual numbing of your senses as you sip on a well-crafted cocktail. The disappearance of local newspapers, the overwhelming flood of national news, and the complacency born of the "it can't happen here" mentality - all of these factors contribute to a landscape where schemes like the one in Pell City can flourish unchecked.

Just as Stacy and Mae refused to be victims of circumstance, we too have the power to change the narrative. Their determination to uncover the truth and seek justice reminds us that individual actions can ripple outward, creating waves of change.

As you set down your empty glass, let the lingering taste of the Alabama Slammer serve as a reminder. A reminder to stay vigilant, to engage with your community, and to look beyond the surface. Often, the most significant narratives unfold within our immediate surroundings.

In the end, the tale of the Alabama Slammer—both the drink and the story—teaches us that appearances can be deceiving. It's up to us to take that first sip, to dig deeper, and to uncover the complex realities that lie beneath.

So the next time you find yourself in a small town, whether it's Pell City or anywhere else, take a moment to look around. Pay attention to the subtle hints, challenge the established norms, and bear in mind: occasionally, the most profound insights emerge from the most unforeseen locations.

And who knows? Maybe you'll be inspired to mix up your own Alabama Slammer - both literally and figuratively. Because in the end, it's not just about the drink in your hand or the story you've heard. It's about the change you choose to make in your world.

Let's toast to that and to the stories that remain untold.

6

BENEATH THE MAGNOLIAS

Act 1. The Spirits: Pink Lady

As the sun dipped below the horizon in Thompson, Georgia, Sarah Mitchell found herself in need of a stiff drink. The newly appointed 4H officer couldn't shake the feeling that something was terribly wrong with this picturesque Southern town. Seeking solace and inspiration, she decided to craft a cocktail that matched the eerie beauty of the twilight hour: a Pink Lady. Little did she know that this delicate concoction would be her last moment of peace before plunging into the dark heart of Thompson's secrets.

As the sun dips below the horizon, painting the sky in shades of blush and rose, you find yourself inspired to create a cocktail that captures the essence of this delicate twilight hour. Your mind settles on the perfect choice: a pink lady.

You begin by selecting a chilled coupe glass from your freezer, its frosted surface promising to keep your creation icy cold. As you place it on the counter, it leaves a ring of condensation, like a halo for the drink to come.

First, you reach for your cocktail shaker. The cool metal feels smooth in your hands as you fill it with ice, the cubes clinking against each other in anticipation.

Now for the star ingredients. You start with gin, its botanical aroma filling the air as you pour a generous measure into the shaker. The clear liquid pools at the bottom, waiting to be transformed.

Next comes applejack, a spirit with a rich history and complex flavor. As you add it to the shaker, you can almost taste the crisp apple notes mingling with the gin's juniper.

For sweetness and color, you reach for the grenadine. Its deep crimson hue promises to turn your cocktail into a blushing beauty. You pour it carefully, watching as it swirls and mixes with the other spirits.

Now, add a hint of tartness to counterbalance the sweetness. You squeeze fresh lemon juice directly into the shaker, and the citrus scent is bright and invigorating.

With all the ingredients assembled, you secure the lid on your shaker. With a fluid motion, you begin to shake. As you move, the ice rattles rhythmically, chilling and combining the flavors into a harmonious blend.

After a vigorous shake, you can feel the shaker grow cold in your hands. It's time. You strain the cocktail into your waiting coupe glass, admiring the way the pale pink liquid cascades smoothly, creating a perfect, silky surface.

For the finishing touch, you decide to add a delicate garnish. You select a bright red maraschino cherry, skewering it gently on a cocktail pick. With a steady hand, you balance it on the rim of the glass; its deep red is a striking contrast to the drink's pastel pink.

You step back to admire your creation. The Pink Lady

stands before you, elegant and inviting. Its soft pink color catches the last light of day, seeming to glow from within the glass.

As you lift the drink to your lips, the aroma hits you first: a complex bouquet of gin botanicals, apple, and a hint of sweet cherry. The first sip is a revelation. The gin provides a sturdy backbone, while the applejack adds depth and warmth. The grenadine's sweetness is perfectly balanced by the lemon's tartness, creating a smooth, well-rounded flavor that dances on your tongue.

In this moment, you realize you've created more than just a cocktail. This Pink Lady is a sensory experience—a perfect balance of flavors and visual appeal. It's a reminder of the art of mixology, how a few carefully chosen ingredients can come together to create something truly special.

As you settle into your favorite chair, Pink Lady in hand, you can't help but feel a sense of accomplishment. This isn't just a drink - it's a celebration of elegance, a toast to the softer side of cocktail craftsmanship. With each sip, you savor not just the flavors but the moment itself, perfectly captured in a glass as delicate and beautiful as the twilight that inspired it.

As Sarah savored the last sips of her Pink Lady, a sudden chill ran down her spine. The elegant cocktail, with its soft pink hue and perfect balance of flavors, seemed to mock the sinister undercurrents she'd begun to sense in Thompson. Setting down the empty glass, Sarah steeled herself for what lay ahead. The Pink Lady had been a momentary escape, a fleeting reminder of beauty and refinement. But now, as storm clouds gathered both literally and figuratively, Sarah knew she was about to be drawn into a mystery far darker than she could have imagined – one where Southern hospitality masked unspeakable horrors, and where the Garden

Club's true nature would soon be revealed. Inspired by my experiences during site visits for the Georgia Trust, this thrilling tale weaves together elements of Southern Gothic horror and small-town mystery. "The Garden Club of Thompson" takes readers on a journey into the dark heart of a seemingly idyllic Georgia town, where appearances are deceiving and Southern hospitality masks sinister secrets.

Sarah Mitchell, a newly arrived 4H officer, finds herself drawn into a web of intrigue centered around the town's Garden Club - a group of elegant elderly women who are far more than they appear. As a storm gathers both literally and figuratively, Sarah uncovers a generations-old conspiracy that has kept the town of Thompson thriving through unspeakable means.

This story blends the charm of small-town Southern life with spine-tingling horror, creating a unique and captivating read. It explores themes of tradition, power, and the lengths some will go to preserve their way of life. Perfect for fans of Southern Gothic literature, horror enthusiasts, or anyone who enjoys a good mystery with a supernatural twist.

Take a moment to immerse yourself in this chilling tale that will make you think twice about accepting an invitation to tea in a quaint Georgia town. It's a testament to the power of a preservationist's imagination, where historic sites become the backdrop for stories that are as haunting as they are entertaining.

Act 2. The Story: The Garden Club's Secret

The summer heat hung heavy over Thompson, Georgia, a small town nestled in the heart of McDuffie County. To the casual observer, it appeared no different from countless other rural communities dotting the Southern landscape – a place where time seemed to move a little slower, where everyone knew their neighbors, and where the biggest excitement usually came from the annual county fair.

But appearances can be deceiving.

Sarah Mitchell, the newly appointed 4H officer for the region, couldn't shake the feeling that something was off as she drove her dusty sedan down Main Street. She'd arrived in Thompson just three weeks ago, eager to make a difference in the lives of local youth. Now, as she passed by the quaint storefronts and waved to a few familiar faces, an inexplicable unease settled in her stomach.

IT HAD STARTED WITH WHISPERS. The hushed conversations abruptly ceased when she entered a room. worried glances were exchanged between longtime residents. Then there were the missing persons posters – far too many for a town this size.

SARAH PULLED into the parking lot of the local diner, hoping a cup of coffee might calm her nerves. As she stepped out of her car, a gust of wind nearly knocked her off balance. She looked up at the darkening sky, frowning at the storm clouds gathering on the horizon.

Inside the diner, the usual buzz of conversation was noticeably subdued. Sarah slid into a booth near the window, nodding a greeting to Mrs. Henderson, the owner, who approached with a steaming pot of coffee.

"Mornin', Sarah," Mrs. Henderson said, her lined face creasing into a forced smile. "The usual?"

"Please," Sarah replied, studying the older woman's face.

There were dark circles under Mrs. Henderson's eyes, and her hands trembled slightly as she poured the coffee. "Everything okay, Mrs. H? You look like you haven't been sleeping well."

Mrs. Henderson's smile faltered for a moment before she quickly composed herself. "Oh, you know how it is, dear. I'm just busy with the diner and all that. Nothing to worry about."

But there was worry in her voice and fear in her eyes. Before Sarah could press further, the bell above the door chimed. A hush fell over the diner as five elderly women entered, all impeccably dressed despite the oppressive heat.

"The Garden Club," Mrs. Henderson whispered, almost to herself. She straightened up, plastering on another smile. "If you'll excuse me, dear."

Sarah watched as Mrs. Henderson hurried to greet the newcomers, noting how the other patrons seemed to shrink in their seats. The women, led by a tall, silver-haired lady with piercing blue eyes, moved with an air of authority that seemed at odds with their floral dresses and pearls.

As they settled into a large corner booth, Sarah couldn't help but overhear snippets of their conversation.

"...another one last night..."

"...the mansion is nearly ready..."

"...full moon approaching..."

A chill ran down Sarah's spine, despite the warmth of the diner. She had a sudden, irrational urge to flee – to pack up her meager belongings and leave Thompson in her rearview mirror. But she was here for a reason, wasn't she? She wanted to help this community and make a difference. She realized she was about to plunge into a mystery far darker and more dangerous than anything she could have imagined as she sipped her coffee and tried to make sense of the strange atmosphere in the diner. The storm clouds gathering outside were nothing compared to the tempest brewing within the seemingly idyllic town of Thompson, Georgia.

And at the center of it all stood a grand old mansion, its Greek revival columns stark against the darkening sky, waiting to reveal its terrible secrets.

The Azalea Room at the Thompson Country Club was a vision of Southern elegance. Delicate china teacups clinked softly against saucers, and the scent of freshly baked scones wafted through the air. At the center of it all were the five women Sarah had seen at the diner, each a picture of grace and refinement.

Eugenia Beaumont, the silver-haired matriarch of the group, adjusted her pearl necklace as she addressed the gathering. "Ladies, I do declare this might be our most successful season yet," she drawled, her voice as smooth as honey. "Why, just last week, we had the pleasure of hosting that charming economic development officer from Atlanta."

Mildred Covington, a petite woman with perfectly coiffed white hair, tittered behind her hand. "Oh, Eugenia, he was quite taken with your peach cobbler. Such a shame he had to leave so... abruptly."

The women exchanged knowing glances, their eyes glittering with secrets.

"Now, now," chided Eugenia, "let's not get ahead of ourselves. We still have several distinguished guests to welcome before our grand soirée at Magnolia Manor."

As if on cue, the door to the Azalea Room opened, and a harried-looking man in a rumpled suit entered. "I'm so sorry I'm late," he stammered, "I'm afraid I got a bit turned around on these country roads."

Eugenia rose, her smile dazzling. "Why, Mr. Hawkins,

you're right on time. Ladies, please welcome Christopher Hawkins from the Georgia Department of Economic Development."

The women cooed and fussed over Christopher, ushering him to a seat and pressing a cup of sweet tea into his hands. He looked a bit overwhelmed by the attention but was nonetheless pleased.

"We're just thrilled you could join us, Mr. Hawkins," said Lucille Fairchild, a statuesque woman with auburn hair. "We so rarely get the chance to discuss economic opportunities with someone of your... expertise."

Christopher straightened his tie, clearly flattered. "Well, I'm always happy to help. Thompson has so much potential, and with the right investments—"

"Oh, we couldn't agree more," Eugenia interrupted smoothly. "In fact, we have some very exciting plans in the works. But first, you simply must try one of Mildred's famous lavender scones."

As the afternoon wore on, more guests arrived – a renowned painter from Savannah, a bestselling mystery author from Macon, and a young botanist studying rare plant species in the area. The same effusive Southern hospitality greeted each, drawing them into conversations that sparkled with wit and charm.To an outsider, it might have seemed like nothing more than a delightful gathering of local socialites and visiting professionals. But there was an undercurrent of tension—a carefully orchestrated dance of words and gestures that hinted at darker purposes.

Eugenia watched it all with satisfaction, her blue eyes sharp and calculating behind her genteel smile. As the sun began to set, casting long shadows across the manicured lawn outside, she clinked her spoon against her teacup.

"My dears," she announced, "I do believe it's time we

introduced our honored guests to the true jewel of Thompson – Magnolia Manor. The forecast calls for a bit of rain this evening, but I'm sure we won't let a little weather dampen our spirits, will we?"

The other club members murmured their agreement, while the guests looked intrigued, if slightly uncertain.

"Splendid," Eugenia continued. "We'll reconvene at the manor at eight o'clock sharp. And do dress for dinner – we may be in the country, but we're not savages."

As the group began to disperse, Christopher Hawkins approached Eugenia. "Ms. Beaumont, I can't thank you enough for your hospitality. I must admit, when I was assigned this project, I didn't expect such a warm welcome."

Eugenia patted his arm, her touch light but somehow possessive. "My dear Mr. Hawkins, you'll find that we take great pride in our little community. And we so look forward to showing you everything Thompson has to offer."

Her smile never wavered, but for a moment, something cold and predatory flashed in her eyes. Christopher, busy checking his phone for the manor's address, didn't notice. By the time he looked up, Eugenia's mask of Southern charm was firmly back in place.

"Until this evening," she said, giving a little wave as she glided out of the room, leaving behind a lingering scent of magnolias and a growing sense of unease.

The rain came suddenly, with sheets of water driven by howling winds that bent the trees and rattled Magnolia Manor's windows. Inside, the guests huddled in the grand parlor, their earlier ease replaced by nervous glances and uncomfortable silence.

Christopher Hawkins stood by a towering window, watching lightning split the sky. "Quite a storm," he muttered, more to himself than anyone else.

"Oh, it's just a little summer squall," Eugenia said, appearing at his elbow. "Nothing to fret about. Now, who'd like a tour of the manor?"

Before anyone could respond, a deafening crack of thunder shook the house to its foundations. The lights flickered once, twice, and then plunged the room into darkness.

Gasps and nervous laughter filled the air. "Stay calm, everyone," Eugenia's voice rang out, unnaturally clear in the sudden quiet. "We're quite prepared for these little power outages."

As if on cue, pinpricks of light began to appear throughout the vast house. From every shadowy corner and every hidden doorway, figures emerged carrying candles and oil lamps. The gentle ladies who had served tea and scones just hours before now moved with eerie purpose, their faces transformed by the flickering flames.

"Ladies," Eugenia commanded, "if you would be so kind as to escort our guests to the grand hall."

The professionals found themselves gently but firmly guided through winding corridors and down creaking staircases. The storm raged outside, but within the manor, an unnatural calm had settled.

Sarah Mitchell, who had arrived late and separated from the group, found herself alone in a dim hallway. She could hear chanting coming from somewhere below – a low, rhythmic sound that seemed to vibrate through the very walls of the house. As she crept towards the sound's source, her curiosity warred with fear.

In the grand hall, Christopher and the others stood in stunned silence. An enormous chalk star marked the floor, with flickering candles at each point. The ladies of the Garden Club formed a circle around it, replacing their floral dresses with flowing black robes.

"What is the meaning of this?" the painter from Savannah demanded, his voice shrill with panic.

Eugenia stepped forward, her silver hair gleaming in the candlelight. "My dears," she said, her honeyed tones now edged with something ancient and terrible, "welcome to the true heart of Thompson. For generations, we have sustained our little community through... shall we say, unconventional means."

"You're insane," Christopher gasped, backing away. "We'll report you to the authorities!"

Eugenia's laugh was like breaking glass. "Oh, Mr. Hawkins. Who do you think sends you to us? Why do you think no one ever comes looking?"

As the chanting grew louder, the candles flared impossibly high. The guests tried to run, only to find their limbs growing heavy and their minds clouding.

From her hidden vantage point, Sarah watched in horror as the scene unfolded. She saw Christopher and the others collapse to the ground, and she saw the robed women converge on them with glinting objects in their hands. She wanted to scream, to run, to do something – but fear kept her rooted to the spot.

Just then, a gnarled hand clamped over her mouth. Sarah tried to struggle, but a familiar voice whispered in her ear, "Hush, child. It's not your time yet."

Mrs. Henderson came from the diner, her eyes wide and wild in the darkness.

With surprising strength, Mrs. Henderson shoved Sarah towards a hidden door. Sarah found herself in the howling wind and rain as it swung shut behind her. The manor loomed behind her like a malevolent shadow.

She ran, branches whipping her face and mud sucking at her feet. She ran until her lungs burned and her legs gave out. She could still hear the chanting and see the unholy light of those candles behind her eyes.

Sarah Mitchell was the one who lived to tell the tale. But as she huddled in her car, speeding away from Thompson, she wondered if anyone would believe her. In the rearview mirror, lightning illuminated Magnolia Manor one last time – a place of genteel evil where Southern hospitality masked an ancient, insatiable hunger.

The storm raged on, washing away the evidence of what had transpired that night. And in Thompson, Georgia, life would go on as it always had – peaceful, picturesque, and harboring secrets darker than the storm-tossed night.

Act 3. The Ponderance: When Leaders Cast Too Long a Shadow

In the world of community development and historic preservation, we often encounter unexpected challenges. Sometimes, these challenges stem not from a lack of resources or interest but from the lingering influence of past leadership. My recent experience with preservation efforts near Thompson, Georgia, brought this issue into sharp focus.

As I delved into strategies to save an endangered historic site in the area, I encountered a peculiar obstacle. The community seemed paralyzed, unable to move forward without the input of a once-prominent leader. The catch? This individual was now residing in an assisted living facility, battling advanced dementia.

The situation was both fascinating and frustrating. Here was a person who had been so influential in decision-making that, even in her absence, her perceived authority cast a long shadow over the community. People were reluctant to take action, fearing potential repercussions or disapproval from this former leader.

This scenario illuminated a critical issue in organizational leadership: the danger of becoming overly reliant on a single individual. When one person becomes the sole decision-maker or the primary driving force behind an organization's efforts, several problems can arise:

1. Stagnation: Without the leader's input, progress grinds to a halt.

2. Loss of diverse perspectives: Other voices and ideas are suppressed or ignored.

3. Vulnerability: The organization becomes overly dependent on one person's vision and abilities.

4. Difficulty in succession: When the leader departs, there's often a leadership vacuum.

As leaders, we must acknowledge that our ultimate goal should be the success and longevity of our projects and organizations, not the perpetuation of our personal influence. This realization leads to several key lessons:

1.Empower others: Encourage team members to take on leadership roles and make decisions.

2.Foster open dialogue: Create an environment where all voices are heard and valued.

3. Develop systems: Implement processes that can function independently of any single individual.

4. Plan for succession: Actively prepare the next generation of leaders.

5. Embrace change: Recognize that new leadership can bring fresh perspectives and ideas.

In the case of the endangered historic site near Thompson, breaking free from the shadow of past leadership was critical for progress. By fostering open dialogue and encouraging new voices, we began to see movement in our preservation efforts.

As leaders, our greatest legacy isn't in maintaining control, but in nurturing an organization that can thrive without us. By empowering others and creating systems that outlast our tenure, we ensure that the valuable work we've started can continue long after we've moved on.

In the end, true leadership is about building something greater than ourselves – a community, an organization, or a cause that can stand the test of time, just like the sturdy walls of the historic structures we seek to preserve.

The satirical story of Thompson's Garden Club serves as a potent illustration of this principle. Just as the town was held hostage by the insidious influence of Eugenia Beaumont and her cohorts, so too can well-intentioned but overly dominant leaders inadvertently stifle the growth and progress of their communities. The tale reminds us that even the most charismatic and seemingly benevolent leadership can cast shadows that linger long after their time has passed.

By recognizing these dangers and actively working to distribute power and responsibility, we can create resilient communities and organizations that are capable of weathering any storm – metaphorical or otherwise. In doing so, we ensure that our efforts in community development and historic preservation create legacies that truly stand the test of time.

7

WHISPERS OF THE PAST

Act 1. The Spirits: Vodka Stinger

As I sipped the crisp Vodka Stinger, its minty coolness a stark contrast to the warmth of the evening, I couldn't shake the memory that had been haunting me for years. It was a tale born from what should have been a routine visit, a simple consultation for a young couple restoring a rural 18th-century house. As a Historic Preservationist, I'd seen my share of old homes, each with its own story to tell. But this one... this one was different. The house had wormed its way into my subconscious, manifesting in a vivid and terrifying dream that had never truly left me. Now, as the icy cocktail numbed my lips, I felt compelled to share this chilling story—a cautionary tale of restoration gone wrong, of history awakening in the most horrifying way imaginable. So settle in, dear reader, and prepare yourself for 'The House of Bees.' But first, perhaps check your surroundings for any unexpected buzzing...

As the evening settles in and the city lights begin to

twinkle, you find yourself in the mood for something classic yet bracing. The answer comes to you in a flash: a Vodka stutter, the perfect blend of smooth and sharp.

You begin by selecting a sleek martini glass from your collection. Its V-shaped silhouette promises elegance and sophistication. You place it in the freezer for a quick chill while you gather your ingredients.

First, you reach for your cocktail shaker. The weight in your hand feels reassuring as you fill it generously with ice cubes. Their crystalline surfaces catch the light, hinting at the frosty concoction to come.

Now for the star of the show—the vodka. You choose a premium bottle whose contents are as clear as mountain spring water. With a steady hand, you pour two and a half ounces over the ice, watching as it cascades down and embraces the frozen cubes.

Next comes the crème de menthe. You've opted for the white variety to maintain the cocktail's clarity. As you uncap the bottle, a burst of cool peppermint fills the air. You measure out a half ounce and add it to the shaker; its syrupy consistency is a stark contrast to the crisp vodka.

With all the ingredients assembled, you secure the lid on your shaker. In one fluid motion, you begin to shake. The ice rattles rhythmically as you move, chilling the liquors and melding their flavors into a harmonious blend. The shaker grows cold in your hands, frosting over slightly—a promise of the icy refreshment within.

After a vigorous thirty-second shake, it's time for the reveal. You retrieve your chilled martini glass from the freezer, its surface misty with frost. With practiced ease, you strain the cocktail into the waiting glass. The liquid pours out smooth and clear, with just a hint of cloudiness from the vigorous shake.

For a finishing touch, you decide to add a subtle garnish. You pluck a single, perfect mint leaf from your herb garden. With a gentle slap between your palms to release its oils, you float it on the surface of the drink. Its vibrant green is a striking contrast to the crystal-clear cocktail.

You step back to admire your handiwork. The Vodka Stinger stands before you, elegant and inviting. The glass frosts over slightly, promising an ice-cold first sip.

As you lift the glass to your lips, the aroma hits you first—a bracing blend of crisp vodka and cool peppermint. The first taste is a revelation. The vodka provides a smooth, clean base, while the crème de menthe adds a refreshing, minty kick that awakens your senses. The chill of the drink is invigorating, perfect for cutting through the warmth of the evening.

In this moment, you realize you've crafted more than just a cocktail. This Vodka Stinger is a sensory journey, a perfect balance of strength and freshness. It's a reminder of the beauty of simplicity in mixology, how two well-chosen ingredients can create something truly memorable.

As you settle into your favorite spot by the window, Vodka Stinger in hand, you can't help but feel a sense of satisfaction. This isn't just a drink - it's a crisp, cool interlude in your evening, a moment of refined refreshment. With each sip, you savor not just the flavors but the moment itself, perfectly captured in a glass as clear and bracing as the night air.

I have a story that's been haunting me for years.

It all began with what seemed like a routine visit to a young couple who had just purchased a rural late-18th-century house. As a historic preservationist, I was there to advise them on restorations. The house was a magnificent example of period architecture, full of history and character.

But little did I know that this visit would leave me with more than just professional observations.

That night, after returning home, I had a dream so vivid and terrifying that it's stayed with me ever since. In my dream, I saw the young mother sitting in a rocking chair in the house's parlor. The scene was eerily quiet at first, but then... I was suddenly attacked by a swarm of bees. I woke up in a cold sweat, the buzzing still echoing in my ears.

This dream, born from a simple house visit, sparked a story in my mind - a tale of a family's dream home turning into a nightmare. It's a story of history coming alive in the most terrifying way, of the thin line between restoration and awakening something that should have remained dormant.

So, , settle in, perhaps check your rooms for any unexpected buzzing, and prepare yourselves for 'The House of Bees.' Remember, sometimes the most chilling tales are born from the most ordinary experiences...

Act 2. The Tale: The Bee House

Sarah Matthews had always been a dreamer. Even as a child, she would spend hours poring over history books, imagining herself living in different eras. Her favorite daydreams were always set in the 18th century, with its elegant dresses, candlelit rooms, and air of mystery. So when she and her husband, Mark, stumbled upon the listing for an 18th-century house nestled in the woods between Athens, Georgia, and Lake Hartwell, it felt like destiny.

The realtor's description was sparse: "Historic 18th-century home, needs restoration. A hidden gem for the right buyer." There was only one grainy photo, showing a weathered facade partially obscured by overgrown vines. But for Sarah, it was love at first sight.

Mark was hesitant at first. "Honey, are you sure about this? It's in the middle of nowhere, and with your health..." His voice trailed off, his eyes flickering to the ports protruding from Sarah's chest – a constant reminder of her ongoing battle with lupus.

But Sarah's eyes sparkled with a determination he hadn't seen in years. "This is our chance, Mark. I want to give Emma the childhood I always dreamed of and leave her with something special. Please?"

How could he resist? Despite his practical nature, Mark had always been putty in Sarah's hands. And if this old house could bring some joy into her life and make her forget about the pain and the endless treatments, even for a little while, then it was worth every penny.

The day they first visited the property, it was unseasonably warm for early spring. Their realtor, a chatty woman named Bethany, prattled on about the house's history as they bumped down the winding dirt road.

"It's been empty for years," Bethany explained, her voice tinged with both excitement and a hint of something else – caution, perhaps? "The last owners were an elderly couple who passed away about a decade ago. Their children tried to sell it, but, well, you know how it is with these old places. They need a special kind of buyer."

As they rounded the final bend, the house came into view. Sarah gasped, her hand instinctively reaching for Mark's. It was grander than she had imagined – a two-story structure with a wide front porch, its white paint peeling to reveal the weathered wood beneath. Thick vines of wisteria climbed the walls, their purple blooms adding splashes of color to the faded exterior.

"It's perfect," Sarah whispered, her eyes wide with wonder.

Mark squeezed her hand, pushing down his own apprehensions. The house did have a certain charm, he had to admit. But there was something else, a feeling he couldn't quite shake – as if the empty windows were watching them, evaluating their worth.

Two-year-old Emma squirmed in her car seat, her chubby hands reaching towards the house. "Home?" she asked, her voice small and curious.

Sarah turned to her daughter, beaming. "Yes, sweetheart. This might be our new home."

As they explored the interior, Sarah's excitement only grew. The rooms were spacious, with high ceilings and ornate moldings. Yes, restoring it to its former glory would require a significant amount of work, but Sarah could already envision its stunning beauty. It was in the library that they made the discovery that sealed the deal. Mark was examining the fireplace, running his hand along the intricate carvings on the mantel, when he felt a slight give. There was a soft click, and a section of the bookcase swung open, revealing a hidden door.

"Sarah, Emma, come look at this!" he called, his earlier reservations momentarily forgotten in the thrill of discovery.

They crowded into the small, musty room beyond. It was barely larger than a closet, but what caught their attention were the walls. After years of dust and cobwebs, they could make out the faded patterns of 18th-century wallpaper – delicate flowers and vines intertwined with what looked like tiny, stylized bees.

Sarah's breath caught in her throat. "It's... it's incredible," she whispered, reaching out to touch the fragile paper. "Mark, do you know what this means? This room – it's been untouched for centuries. It's like a time capsule."

Mark watched his wife's face, saw the color in her cheeks and the light in her eyes that had been missing for so long. In that moment, he knew they would buy the house, whatever the cost.

As they signed the papers a week later, none of them noticed the strange shimmer in the air or the faint buzzing sound that seemed to emanate from the walls. The house had chosen its new occupants, and it was eager to welcome them home.

Little did the Matthews family know that their dream home harbored dark secrets, waiting to be awakened by their presence. The whispers on the walls were just the beginning.

The weeks following the purchase were a whirlwind of activity. Mark took a leave of absence from his job as a software engineer to focus on the house's restoration. Sarah threw herself into researching the property's history, spending hours online and in local libraries, piecing together the house's past.

"It was built in 1784 by a wealthy plantation owner named Ezekiel Hawthorne," Sarah explained one evening as they sat on the porch, watching the sunset paint the sky in hues of orange and pink. "He was known for his... unusual interests."

Mark raised an eyebrow, pausing in his task of rocking Emma to sleep. "Unusual how?"

Sarah hesitated, her fingers tracing the outline of the port in her chest – a nervous habit she'd developed since her diagnosis. "Well, according to some accounts, he was obsessed with the idea of immortality. There are rumors that he conducted experiments, trying to find a way to cheat death."

A chill ran down Mark's spine, despite the warm evening air. "Experiments? What kind of experiments?"

Sarah shrugged, her excitement about the house's history overriding any sense of unease. "It's probably just local legend. You know how people love to embellish these old stories."

As the days passed, the house slowly began to transform. Mark focused on the structural repairs, while Sarah, on her good days, worked on restoring the intricate moldings and choosing historically accurate paint colors. The hidden room became Sarah's pet project. She spent hours carefully cleaning the delicate wallpaper, revealing more of the intricate bee pattern with each passing day.

It was during one of these cleaning sessions that Sarah first noticed something odd. As she worked, she could have sworn she heard a faint buzzing sound coming from within the walls. At first, she dismissed it as her imagination, or perhaps a trick of the old house's acoustics. But as the days went by, the sound seemed to grow louder and more insistent.

One afternoon, as Sarah was taking a break from her work in the hidden room, she noticed Emma staring intently at a corner of the ceiling.

"What is it, sweetie?" Sarah asked, following her daughter's gaze.

Emma pointed a chubby finger upward. "Bees, Mommy. Bees go buzz-buzz."

Sarah felt a chill run down her spine. There were no bees in the room – she would have noticed them during her meticulous cleaning. And yet, after Emma had mentioned it, she could hear that faint buzzing sound again, seeming to emanate from the very walls themselves.

"There are no bees, honey," Sarah said, trying to keep her

voice light. "It's just an old house. Sometimes old houses make funny noises."

But even as she spoke the words, Sarah couldn't shake the feeling that there was more to it than that. That night, as she lay in bed beside Mark, she found herself unable to sleep, the memory of that buzzing sound echoing through her mind.

It was just past midnight when Sarah bolted upright, her heart pounding. The buzzing was back, louder than ever, and it seemed to be coming from everywhere at the same time. She shook Mark awake, her voice trembling.

"Mark, do you hear that?"

Mark blinked groggily, then sat up, suddenly alert. "Hear what?"

But as quickly as it had come, the sound faded away, leaving behind an eerie silence.

"It... it was like a swarm of bees," Sarah whispered, clutching the blanket to her chest. "All around us, in the walls."

Mark wrapped an arm around her and furrowed his brow with concern. "It was probably just a dream, honey. You've been working so hard on the house, and with your condition..."

Sarah nodded, willing herself to believe him. But as she settled back into bed, she couldn't shake the feeling that something in the house had awakened – something that was now acutely aware of their presence.

The next morning, as Sarah made her way downstairs, she noticed something that made her blood run cold. On the wall of the main hallway, there was a single, perfect honeycomb, glistening with fresh honey. And as she watched, frozen in place, a single bee emerged from a tiny crack in the woodwork, its wings buzzing ominously in the morning silence.

Sarah blinked, and in that instant, both the honeycomb and the bee vanished, leaving behind only the faded wallpaper and the creaking of old floorboards. But Sarah knew what she had seen, and the implications sent a shiver of fear through her body.

The house was evolving and awakening, and Sarah had a sinking feeling that their dream home was about to become a nightmare.

As spring gave way to summer, the Matthews family settled into a routine, but an undercurrent of unease permeated their daily lives. Sarah's lupus flared up more frequently, leaving her bedridden for days at a time. Mark struggled to balance his concern for his wife with the seemingly endless repairs the house required. And little Emma, once a bundle of energy and laughter, grew quieter, often finding herself whispering to unseen companions in empty corners of the house.

It was on one particularly stifling Georgia night that things took a turn for the worse. Sarah woke with a start, her nightgown drenched in sweat. The bedroom was stiflingly hot, despite the air conditioning running at full blast. As she reached for the glass of water on her nightstand, she froze. The far wall, illuminated by the pale moonlight filtering through the curtains, was a sight that made her blood run cold.

The wallpaper was changing.

Tiny flowers and vines seemed to writhe and twist, and within their patterns, Sarah could make out the unmistakable shapes of bees, swarming in intricate formations. She blinked hard, convinced she must be hallucinating – a side effect of her medication, perhaps. But when she opened her eyes, the wall was still alive with movement.

"Mark," she whispered, her voice hoarse with fear. "Mark, wake up!"

But as she turned to shake her husband awake, she realized with horror that the bed beside her was empty. In fact, the entire room had changed. Gone was their carefully restored bedroom with its modern comforts. Instead, Sarah found herself in what appeared to be an 18th-century bedchamber, complete with a roaring fire in the hearth and heavy, brocade curtains at the windows.

The buzzing grew louder, filling her ears with its incessant drone. Sarah scrambled out of bed, her heart pounding. "Mark! Emma!" she cried, stumbling towards the door.

As her hand touched the ornate brass doorknob, a voice behind her made her freeze.

"They can't hear you, my dear. Not anymore."

Sarah turned slowly, her breath catching in her throat. There, seated in a high-backed chair by the fire, was a man she had never seen before – and yet, somehow, she knew exactly who he was.

Ezekiel Hawthorne smiled, his eyes glittering in the firelight. He was dressed in late 18th-century fashion, his powdered wig slightly askew, revealing wisps of gray hair beneath. "Welcome home," he said, his voice carrying an otherworldly resonance. "We've been waiting"

Sarah backed away, her hand fumbling for the doorknob behind her. "This isn't real," she muttered. "It's a dream. It has to be a dream."

Ezekiel's smile widened, As he spoke, the buzzing grew to a deafening roar. The wallpaper seemed to peel away from the walls, revealing a writhing mass of bees beneath.

They poured into the room in an endless stream, swirling around Sarah like a dizzying vortex.

"You and your family," Ezekiel continued, rising from his chair, "are the key to my great work. The final ingredients in my quest for immortality."

Sarah felt a sharp sting at the base of her skull, and then another, and another. The bees attacked her, their venom burning through her veins like liquid fire. She screamed, but the sound was lost in the roar of the swarm.

Just as the darkness began to close in around her, Sarah jolted awake with a gasp. She was back in her own bed, with Mark snoring softly beside her. The room was quiet, save for the gentle hum of the air conditioner.

A dream. It had all been a terrible dream.

But as Sarah's racing heart began to slow, she felt a sharp pain at the base of her skull. Reaching back with trembling fingers, she felt a small, hard lump – unmistakably a bee sting.

And, somewhere deep within the old house's walls, she heard the faintest buzzing echo.

In the days that followed her terrifying night vision, Sarah found herself caught between two realities. By day, she tried to maintain a sense of normalcy, focusing on her family and the house restoration. But each night brought fresh horrors – vivid dreams of Ezekiel Hawthorne and his swarms of bees, always waking to find new stings on her body.

Mark noticed the change in his wife. The light that had returned to her eyes when they first bought the house was fading, replaced by a haunted look he couldn't quite understand. "Maybe we should take a break," he suggested one morning, watching Sarah pick listlessly at her breakfast. "Go stay with your sister for a while until you're feeling better."

But Sarah shook her head vehemently. "No, we can't leave. Not now. There's... there's still so much to do."

She couldn't explain it, even to herself, but Sarah felt an inexplicable pull to the house. It was as if leaving would somehow make things worse and would allow whatever force remained within free rein to grow stronger.

It was Emma who first noticed the changes in the hidden room. "Mommy, the pictures move," she said one afternoon, tugging at Sarah's sleeve.

Sarah followed her daughter into the small space, her heart racing. At first glance, everything seemed normal. But as she watched, she saw it – a subtle shifting in the wallpaper pattern, the tiny painted bees seeming to crawl across the surface.

"It's okay, sweetie," Sarah said, trying to keep her voice steady. "It's just a trick of the light."

But Emma shook her head, eyes wide. "They talk to me, Mommy. The bees. They say they're hungry."

A chill ran down Sarah's spine. Before she could respond, she heard Mark calling from downstairs, his voice tinged with panic.

"Sarah! Come quick!"

She scooped up Emma and hurried down to find Mark in the library, staring at the fireplace in disbelief. They had painstakingly restored the ornate carvings on the mantel, which had changed overnight. Where there had once been delicate floral patterns, there were now grotesque faces twisted in agony, their mouths open in silent screams.

"How... how is this possible?" Mark whispered, reaching out to touch the warped wood.

As his fingers made contact, a shock seemed to run through the house. The lights flickered, and a deep groan emanated from the very foundations.

Suddenly, the air was filled with a deafening buzz. Bees poured from every crack and crevice – hundreds, thousands of them—filling the room in a terrifying swarm.

"Run!" Sarah screamed, clutching Emma close to her chest as she bolted for the door.

Act 3. The Ponderance: Do Places Have Memories?

In our journey through life, we often encounter spaces that seem to resonate with palpable energy—a sense of history, emotion, or experience that lingers long after the events that shaped them have passed. This phenomenon, often described as "place memory," suggests that physical locations can retain and transmit the essence of past occurrences.

As we explore historic sites, from ancient ruins to more recent locations marked by significant events, many of us have felt an inexplicable connection to the past. The weathered stones of a medieval castle might whisper tales of long-ago battles, while the somber atmosphere of Holocaust death camps can evoke a profound sense of sorrow and reverence.

But is this merely our imagination at work, or is there something more tangible at play?

While the idea of places having memories isn't scientifically proven in a literal sense, several fields of study offer insights that might explain why we perceive certain locations as having a unique "energy" or atmosphere:

1. Collective Memory: Sociologist Maurice Halbwachs introduced the concept of "collective memory," suggesting that groups of people can share and transmit memories associated with specific places. This shared narrative can influence how we perceive and interact with these locations.

2. Environmental Psychology: This field examines how physical environments affect human behavior and well-being. Studies have shown that the design, history, and cultural significance of a place can influence our emotional responses and cognitive processes.

3. Architectural Phenomenology: Philosophers and architects like Christian Norberg-Schulz have explored how the character of a place (its "genius loci" or spirit of place) can be shaped by its physical features and cultural associations.

4. Psychogeography: This approach, developed by Guy Debord, investigates the emotional and behavioral impacts of geographical environments on individuals.

5. Epigenetics and Transgenerational Trauma: While controversial, some researchers suggest that traumatic experiences can leave epigenetic marks on DNA that can be passed down through generations. This could potentially explain why some people feel a strong emotional connection to places associated with their ancestors' experiences.

While these theories don't prove that places literally have memories, they do offer explanations for why we might perceive them as such. The energy we feel in historic locations could be a combination of our knowledge of past events, the physical characteristics of the space, and our own emotional and cultural associations.

As we stand in places of great historical significance—be it the awe-inspiring grandeur of ancient temples or the solemn grounds of concentration camps—we become part of a continuing narrative. We add our own experiences and emotions to the tapestry of human history that is woven into these locations.

In the end, whether places truly have memories or not, our perception of them as repositories of history and emotion shapes our understanding of the world and our place in it. By recognizing and respecting the power of these spaces, we honor the experiences of those who came before us and create meaningful connections between the past, present, and future.

Collective memory, a concept introduced by French sociologist Maurice Halbwachs, suggests that memories can be shared, passed down, and maintained by groups of people. This theory has significant implications for how we perceive places with rich histories.

Collective memory can be particularly strong in locations where significant events occurred. For example, battlefields, natural disaster sites, or places of cultural importance often carry a weight of shared memories that can be felt by visitors, even those with no direct connection to the events.

The idea of collective memory could explain why certain places gain reputations for being haunted. As stories and experiences are shared within a community, they become part of the collective consciousness, potentially influencing how future visitors perceive and interact with the space. This shared narrative might lead people to interpret ambiguous stimuli as paranormal experiences, reinforcing the location's reputation as haunted.

Environmental psychology examines the interplay between humans and their surroundings, including how physical spaces affect our behavior, emotions, and well-being.

Studies in this field have shown that factors such as lighting, acoustics, temperature, and spatial layout can significantly impact our mood and perception. Historic places often have unique environmental characteristics that can trigger strong emotional responses. For example, the dim lighting and cool temperatures in old castles might elicit feelings of unease or excitement.

The environmental features of allegedly haunted locations often align with factors that psychology has shown to induce unease or altered states of consciousness. Dark, quiet spaces can heighten our sensitivity to small sounds or movements. Old buildings may have unusual acoustic properties that create eerie sounds. These environmental factors could contribute to experiences that people interpret as supernatural.

3. Architectural Phenomenology

This philosophical approach, championed by theorists like Christian Norberg-Schulz, explores how the character or "spirit" of a place (genius loci) is shaped by its physical and cultural attributes.

Architectural phenomenology suggests that places have a unique identity formed by their physical features, cultural associations, and the experiences they facilitate. This identity can evoke specific emotions and behaviors in people who interact with the space.

Places reputed to be haunted often have strong identities shaped by their history and physical characteristics. The imposing architecture of a Gothic mansion or the isolated setting of an abandoned asylum contributes to their eerie atmosphere. These strong place identities might predispose visitors to expect or experience supernatural phenomena.

Psychogeography, a concept developed by Guy Debord and the Situationist International, psychogeography investigates how geographical environments influence people's emotions and behaviors.

Psychogeography encourages a new way of exploring urban environments, focusing on the emotional and psychological experiences they provoke. It suggests that the layout of streets, the presence of certain buildings, or the overall ambiance of an area can have subtle but significant effects on our mental state.

The principles of psychogeography could explain why certain areas within cities or landscapes become associated with supernatural activity. The convergence of historical events, architectural features, and urban legends in a specific location might create a psychogeographical "hot spot" where people are more likely to report ghostly encounters.

While this is a more controversial area, some researchers propose that traumatic experiences can leave epigenetic marks on DNA that can be inherited by future generations.

This theory posits that the transmission of severe trauma across generations may occur not only through storytelling or cultural practices, but also potentially through biological mechanisms. Although the research is still in its early stages, it poses intriguing questions about our potential connection to our ancestors' experiences.

If there's validity to the concept of inherited trauma responses, it could provide an alternative explanation for why some individuals feel strong emotional connections to places associated with their ancestors' traumatic experiences. What may be perceived as a ghostly encounter could be an intense emotional response triggered by inherited epigenetic markers.

While these theories don't provide concrete evidence for the existence of ghosts or literal place memories, they offer fascinating insights into why we might perceive certain locations as haunted or imbued with past experiences. The interplay of collective memory, environmental factors, architectural design, urban exploration, and potentially even inherited biological responses creates a complex tapestry of human experience in relation to place.

These perspectives invite us to consider haunted places not just as potential sites of paranormal activity but as rich, multifaceted environments that engage our senses, emotions, and imaginations in profound ways. Whether or not ghosts exist in a literal sense, the power of place to evoke the past and stir deep emotional responses is undeniably real and worthy of continued exploration.

As the last echoes of the Matthews family's terrifying encounter with the House of Bees fade away, we're left to ponder the nature of the world around us. Their story, while fiction, touches upon very real human experiences and fears.

The House of Bees, with its living wallpaper and spectral former owner, may seem far-fetched. Yet, how many of us have walked into an old building and felt a chill run down our spine? How many have sensed an inexplicable presence in a historic location or felt overwhelmed by emotion in a place marked by past tragedies?

Perhaps what we perceive as supernatural is simply our minds grappling with the complex interplay of collective memory, environmental psychology, and the weight of history. The buzzing in the walls of the Matthews' home might be a metaphor for the persistent echoes of the past that resonate in places of significance.

As we've explored, the concept of place memory isn't about literal ghosts or magical properties imbued in bricks and mortar. Rather, it's about the powerful confluence of shared narratives, environmental factors, and our own psychological responses to spaces rich with history and emotion.

In the end, whether we believe in ghosts or not, the

power of place to evoke strong emotions and experiences is undeniable. The House of Bees may be fiction, but the feeling of connection to the past that it represents is very real.

So the next time you find yourself in an old house, a historic battlefield, or any place with a storied past, take a moment to reflect. Listen not for literal whispers from beyond, but for the subtle ways in which the space speaks to you through its architecture, atmosphere, and the weight of the stories it holds.

Understanding these connections allows us to gain a deeper appreciation for the complex tapestry of human experience woven into the very fabric of the places we live. And who knows? You might just hear a faint buzzing in the walls, reminding you that the past never truly disappears; it simply waits for us to listen.

8

THE WHISPERS OF ATHENS

Act 1. The Spirits: Seven and Seven

In the quiet streets of Athens, Georgia, where the past lingers like the scent of magnolias, a tale unfolds that reminds us how love can blind us to reason. Ellen Beaumont, a widow whose world revolves around her son Rodney, finds herself at the center of a storm that begins with a single phone call and ends in a way no one could have predicted.

This story, born from the whispers of local gossip and the fears that haunt us all, takes us on a journey through the heart of a mother's devotion and the dark underbelly of modern scams. It's a tale that could happen to anyone - a reminder that in our interconnected world, danger can reach us even in the safety of our homes.

As we follow Ellen's desperate attempts to save her son from a threat that exists only in her mind, we're forced to ask ourselves: How far would we go to protect the ones we love? And at what point does our desire to help become a danger in itself?

Prepare yourself for a story that blends the warmth of Southern hospitality with the cold reality of criminal manipulation. "The Whispers of Athens" is more than just a cautionary tale - it's a mirror held up to our own fears, hopes, and the unbreakable bonds of family.

As the sun dips below the horizon, you find yourself craving something simple yet satisfying. The answer? A classic Seven and Seven.

You start by selecting a sturdy highball glass from your collection. The weight in your hand feels just right as you begin to fill it with ice cubes, each one clinking against the glass with a satisfying sound.

Next, you reach for the star of the show - a bottle of Seagram's 7 Crown Whiskey. Its amber liquid catches the last rays of sunlight as you pour a generous two ounces over the ice. The whiskey settles, weaving its way through the cracks between the cubes.

Now comes the "seven" in Seven and Seven. You grab a cold bottle of 7 Up from the fridge; its condensation leaves a trail on your countertop. With a practiced hand, you uncap it, releasing a soft hiss of carbonation. Slowly, you pour the 7 Up over the whiskey and ice, watching as it fizzes and froths, creating a perfect harmony of flavors.

As the drink comes together, you notice how the colors blend—the golden whiskey and the clear soda—creating a pale amber concoction that seems to glow from within. You give it a gentle stir with a long spoon, just enough to ensure everything is well mixed without losing too much carbonation.

For a final touch, you decide to add a lemon wedge. You slice into a fresh lemon, its citrusy scent filling the air. You place the wedge on the glass rim, adding a pop of yellow to your creation.

You step back and admire your handiwork. The Seven and Seven stand before you, deceptively simple yet undeniably alluring. Condensation beads are already forming on the outside of the glass, promising a cool, refreshing experience.

As you lift the drink to your lips, you can't help but smile. This unpretentious cocktail, born from just two ingredients, is a testament to the beauty of simplicity. With its perfect balance of smooth whiskey and crisp, bubbly soda, you know that this Seven and Seven is exactly what you need to end your day on a high note.

From the simple pleasures of mixing a perfect Seven and Seven to the complex web of small-town gossip, life's richest moments often arise from the most unexpected places. Just as the whiskey and soda blend to create something greater than the sum of their parts, so too do the whispers and rumors of Athens, Georgia, coalesce into a story that captivates and connects its residents. Both narratives remind us of the power of simplicity—be it in a classic cocktail or a juicy piece of gossip—to bring people together, spark our imaginations, and transform the ordinary into the extraordinary. As we transition from the quiet contemplation of a well-crafted drink to the bustling aisles of a grocery store alive with speculation, we're invited to savor the full spectrum of human experience, from solitary reflection to communal storytelling.

Picture this: There I was minding my own business in the produce aisle of the local grocery store, carefully selecting the perfect avocado for my famous guacamole, when the gossip mill started churning faster than the rotisserie chicken display. Now, I can't reveal my source (a shopper never tells, and neither does a bag boy with an ear for drama), but let's just say this tale spread faster than spilled milk on aisle five. It was like the whole town of Athens, Georgia, had suddenly turned into a game of telephone, with each retelling growing wilder than the last. By the time it reached my eager ears, somewhere between the cereal boxes and the frozen peas, I half expected to hear that Elvis himself had risen from the grave to play a part in this Southern Gothic escapade. So grab your shopping cart and let me spin you a yarn that would make even the most seasoned coupon-clipper drop their weekly specials in shock. The medium of gossip—a story that proves once again that truth can indeed be stranger than fiction.

In the quiet corners of Athens, Georgia, a whisper began. A tale of a mother's love, a son's ambition, and a scam that nearly tore them apart. It's a story that makes us question: What would we do for the ones we love? How far would we go when faced with our deepest fears?

As I share this tale with you, I want you to consider how easily events can transform into legend and lore. How one person's rational decision can be another's folly, and yet, in the South, it all becomes fodder for phone calls filled with intrigue and speculation.

This story, my friends, is a reminder of the power of gossip—that most basic and timeless of human elements. It's the whisper in the wind that has created legends since time immemorial. It's the spark that ignites our imagination and connects us to one another in ways both profound and problematic.

So settle in, , as we embark on this journey through the streets of Athens, into the heart of a mother's fear, and out the other side where reality and perception collide.

Act 2. The Tale: "The Whispers of Athens"

Ellen sat in her favorite armchair, the one with the faded floral pattern that smelled faintly of her late husband's pipe tobacco. The house was quiet, save for the ticking of the grandfather clock in the hallway. It was a sound that used to blend into the background of their busy lives, but now it seemed to echo through the emptiness, marking each lonely second.

She reached for the remote, flicking through channels without really seeing what was on. The TV is just background noise these days, a poor substitute for conversation. Her eyes drifted to the framed photo on the side table—her and Frank on their 40th anniversary cruise. His smile was as bright as ever, even with the gray at his temples. God, how she missed that smile.

The phone rang, startling her out of her reverie. She fumbled for her reading glasses, squinting at the caller ID. Her heart lifted when she saw that it was Rodney.

"Hey there, sugar," she said, unable to keep the smile out of her voice. "How's the Big Apple treating you?"

"It's... something else, Mama," Rodney replied, his voice tinny through the speaker. "I had my audition today. I think it went well, but you never know in this business."

Ellen nodded, even though he couldn't see her. "You just keep your chin up, honey. They'd be fools not to see how talented you are."

They chatted for a while about the sights he'd seen, the interesting people he'd met. Ellen soaked up every word, trying to picture the bustling streets and towering buildings. For sure, it was a far cry from their quiet corner of Athens.

As they were saying their goodbyes, Ellen felt a lump

form in her throat. "You be careful out there, you hear? Call your mama more often. I worry."

Rodney's laugh crackled through the line. "I will, Mama. Love you."

"Love you too, sugar."

The silence after she hung up seemed even more oppressive than before. Ellen sighed, hauling herself out of the chair. Maybe a little fresh air would do her good.

She puttered around in the garden for a bit, deadheading the hydrangeas and pulling a few stubborn weeds. Frank had always teased her about her green thumb, saying she could make a brick sprout if she put her mind to it. The memory brought a sad smile to her face.

As the sun started to dip low in the sky, Ellen headed back inside. She poured herself a Seven and Seven—her favorite drink, though she rarely indulged these days. The whiskey's sweet burn was comforting as she sipped it, settling back into her chair.

She must have dozed off, because the next thing she knew, she was jolted awake by the shrill ring of the phone. Disoriented, she fumbled for it, nearly knocking over her half-empty glass in the process.

"Hello?" she mumbled, her voice thick with sleep.

"Is this Ellen Beaumont?" The voice on the other end was gruff and unfamiliar.

"Yes, this is she. Who's calling, please?"

There was a pause, then: "Ma'am, we have your son."

Ellen's blood ran cold. "I... I'm sorry, what did you say?"

"Your son, Rodney. He is with us. And if you want to see him alive again, you're going to do exactly as we say."

The world seemed to tilt on its axis. Ellen's heart hammered in her chest, her palms suddenly slick with sweat. "This... this has to be some kind of mistake. My Rodney's in New York, he-"

"No mistake, ma'am," the voice cut her off. "Now listen carefully. We need $10,000 in cash. Small bills—nothing larger than twenty. You have 24 hours to get it together."

Ellen's mind raced. This couldn't be happening. It had to be some kind of sick joke. But the cold dread settling in her stomach told her otherwise.

"Please," she whispered, her voice cracking. "Please don't hurt him. He's all I have left."

"That's up to you, ma'am. We'll call back with further instructions. Remember: 24 hours. If you call the police, your boy will be dead. Understood?"

The line went dead before Ellen could respond. She sat there, the phone still clutched to her ear, as the dial tone droned on. Then, as if a switch had been flipped, she burst into action.

Her hands shaking, she dialed Rodney's number. It went straight to voicemail. She tried again. And again. Each time, her panic ratcheted up a notch.

"This isn't happening," she muttered to herself, pacing the living room. "This can't be happening."

She needed to think. She needed another drink.

Ellen stumbled to the liquor cabinet, pouring herself a generous seven and seven. The familiar ritual helped calm her nerves, if only slightly. As she took a long swig, her eyes fell on the framed photo of Frank in his police uniform.

Frank. What would Frank do?

With sudden clarity, Ellen knew exactly what her late husband would say. "Don't let those bastards see you sweat, Ellie. And always call for backup."

Ellen made a decision and grabbed her purse and car keys. The Athens-Clarke County Police Department was only a fifteen-minute drive away. Surely they'd know what to do.

The police station's fluorescent lights were harsh after the dim warmth of her living room. Ellen blinked, disoriented, as she approached the front desk.

"Can I help you, ma'am?" The young officer behind the counter looked barely old enough to shave.

Ellen took a deep breath, trying to keep her voice steady. "My name is Ellen Beaumont. I... I think my son has been kidnapped."

The officer's eyebrows shot up. "That's a serious accusation, ma'am. Can you tell me what happened?"

Ellen recounted the phone call, her voice growing more frantic with each word. By the time she finished, her hands were shaking again.

The officer listened patiently, then held up a hand. "Ma'am, I'm going to ask you to take a deep breath. What you're describing sounds like a common scam we've been seeing a lot of lately."

Ellen blinked. "A... a scam?"

He nodded. "These scammers call people, usually older folks, and claim to have kidnapped a loved one. They demand money, trying to scare people into acting without thinking. But I can assure you, it's not real."

Relief washed over Ellen, quickly followed by embarrassment. "Oh. Oh, I see. I... I feel so foolish."

The officer gave her a kind smile. "Don't feel bad, ma'am. These scammers are professionals. They know exactly what buttons to push. The important thing is you didn't fall for it."

Ellen nodded, gathering her purse. "Thank you, officer. I appreciate your time."

As she drove home, Ellen's embarrassment faded, replaced by anger. How dare they try to prey on people like that? And to use a mother's love for her child... it was despicable.

She was just settling back into her chair, another Seven and Seven in hand, when the phone rang again. Her heart leapt into her throat when she saw it was the same number as before.

Against her better judgment, she answered.

"Hello, Ellen," the gruff voice said. "I hope you've had time to think about our offer."

Ellen's grip tightened on the phone. "Now you listen here," she hissed. "I know this is a scam. The police informed me of everything. So you can just-"

"The police?" The voice turned cold. "I thought I told you what would happen if you went to the police."

There was a muffled sound in the background, then a voice that made Ellen's blood run cold.

"Mama? Mama, help me!"

Rodney was there. There was no mistaking it.

"Oh God," Ellen whispered. "Rodney?"

But the gruff voice was back. "You've made a mistake, Ellen. A very big mistake. But I'm feeling generous. You bring the money to the Little City Diner on Cherokee Road, near Winterville. Tomorrow, 2 p.m. sharp. A car will be waiting. Put the money inside, and maybe - just maybe - you'll see your boy again."

The line went dead.

Ellen sat there, frozen, for what felt like hours. It couldn't be real. The police had said... but she'd heard Rodney. She'd heard her baby boy, scared and calling for her.

With shaking hands, she dialed the police station again.

"Ma'am, we've been over this," the officer said, his

patience clearly wearing thin. "It's a scam. They probably used a voice recording or-"

"You don't understand!" Ellen cut him off. "I heard my Rodney. It was him!"

But no matter how much she pleaded, the officer wouldn't budge. Finally, frustrated and scared, Ellen hung up.

She poured herself another drink, stronger this time. As the whiskey burned its way down her throat, a plan began to form.

If the police wouldn't help her, she'd have to take matters into her own hands.

The next morning dawned bright and clear, a beautiful Georgia spring day that seemed to mock Ellen's inner turmoil. She hadn't slept a wink, her mind racing with possibilities, each more terrifying than the last.

She'd withdrawn the money first thing, cleaning out her savings account and maxing out her credit cards. The bank teller had given her an odd look but hadn't asked any questions.

Now, with trembling hands, she opened the safe hidden in the back of her closet. Frank had always insisted they keep it, "just in case." She'd thought him paranoid at the time, but now...

The Glock felt heavy in her hands. Frank had taught her how to use it, and she practiced at the range until she could consistently hit the target. "Just in case," he'd said again. She'd never imagined "just in case" would look like this.

Ellen tucked the gun into her purse, alongside the stack of bills. Then, steeling herself, she poured one last Seven and Seven for courage.

As she pulled into the parking lot of the Little City Diner, her heart was pounding so hard she thought it might burst out of her chest. She parked near the back, scanning the area for any sign of suspicious activity.

Nothing seemed out of place. Just the usual lunchtime crowd: people going about their day, oblivious to the drama unfolding in their midst.

At exactly 2 PM, a car pulled up beside her. A young woman got out, phone in hand, looking around expectantly.

This was it. This had to be them.

With shaking hands, Ellen reached for her purse. The gun's cool metal was reassuring against her palm.

She took a deep breath, then opened her car door.

"Excuse me," she called out, her voice surprisingly steady. "Are you... are you here for the pickup?"

The young woman turned with a friendly smile on her face. "Oh, hi there! Are you Ellen?"

Ellen nodded, her grip tightening on the gun in her purse.

"Great!" the woman said. "I'm Maria, your Uber driver. Ready to go?"

For a moment, Ellen's mind went blank. Uber driver? But... but the kidnappers...

Then it hit her. They must have used Uber as a cover. Clever bastards.

"Of course," Ellen said, forcing a smile. "Just... just give me one moment."

She fumbled for her phone, dialing 911 with trembling fingers.

"911, what's your emergency?"

"Please," Ellen whispered, keeping an eye on Maria. "I'm at the Little City Diner on Cherokee Road. The kidnappers are here. Please hurry."

"Ma'am, is this Ellen Beaumont again? We've told you-"

Ellen hung up, frustration and fear warring inside her. They weren't going to help. She was on her own.

Taking a deep breath, she turned back to Maria. "I'm so sorry about this, dear," she said, reaching into her purse. "But I'm going to need you to come with me."

Maria's eyes widened as Ellen pulled out the gun. "Whoa, what the hell? Lady, put that down!"

"Get in the car," Ellen said, her voice shaking despite her best efforts. "Now!"

Maria raised her hands, backing away slowly. "Okay, okay, just... just take it easy. You don't want to do this."

"I said get in the car!" Ellen's voice rose to a shout. "I won't let you hurt my Rodney!"

Maria looked confused and terrified. "Who's Rodney? Lady, I'm just an Uber driver! Please, put the gun down!"

However, Ellen was now beyond reason. All she could think about was Rodney, her baby boy, scared and alone. She had to save him. She had to...

The wail of police sirens cut through the air. Ellen spun around to see two patrol cars speeding into the parking lot.

"Freeze! Put the weapon down!"

Ellen blinks, disoriented. This... this wasn't how it was supposed to go. Where were the kidnappers? Where was Rodney?

"I said put the weapon down! Now!"

Slowly, as if in a dream, Ellen lowered the gun. As soon as it left her hand, she was shoved to the ground, the rough asphalt scraping her cheek.

"You're under arrest," a voice said in her ear as cold metal encircled her wrists. "You have the right to remain silent..."

Ellen barely heard the words. All she could think about was Rodney. Oh God, what had she done?

As they led her to the patrol car, she caught sight of Maria talking to another officer, shaken but unharmed.

"Wait," Ellen called out, her voice hoarse. "Please, you don't understand. My son... they have my son!"

But no one was listening. The car door slammed shut, cutting off her pleas.

As they drove away, Ellen slumped in the backseat, the reality of what had just happened crashing down on her. She'd pulled a gun on an innocent woman. She was going to jail. Rodney... oh my God, what about Rodney?

Tears streamed down her face as the Little City Diner faded from view. All she'd wanted was to protect her son. How had everything gone so terribly wrong?

In that moment, as the reality of her situation sank in, Ellen Beaumont had never felt more alone.

The holding cell was cold and sterile, a far cry from the warm comfort of Ellen's living room. She sat on the hard bench, her head in her hands, trying to make sense of the whirlwind that had become her life.

The door clanged open, and Ellen looked up, hope flaring in her chest. Maybe they'd finally listened, maybe they'd found Rodney...

But it wasn't Rodney. It was a tall, distinguished-looking man in a suit, a briefcase in his hand.

"Mrs. Beaumont?" He spoke in a gentle tone. "I'm Charles Dawson, your court-appointed attorney. May I have a seat?"

Ellen nodded numbly. The lawyer settled beside her, opening his briefcase.

"Mrs. Beaumont, I've reviewed your case, and I have to say, it's quite a situation you've found yourself in." He paused, studying her face. "But before we discuss the legal aspects, I need to ask: have you heard from your son?"

Ellen's head snapped up. "Rodney? No, I... the kidnappers, they..."

Mr. Dawson held up a hand. "Mrs. Beaumont, I'm afraid there were no kidnappers. Your son has been in contact with the police. He's fine, he's in New York, auditioning for... a cooking show, I believe?"

The world seemed to tilt on its axis. "But... but I heard him. On the phone, I heard him calling for me."

The lawyer's expression was sympathetic. "I'm afraid that was likely a recording, or perhaps someone imitating your son's voice. These scammers are unfortunately very skilled at manipulation."

Ellen felt the last bit of fight drain out of her. It had all been for nothing. She'd terrorized an innocent woman, gotten herself arrested... and Rodney had been safe the whole time.

"Oh God," she whispered, fresh tears welling up. "What have I done?"

As news of Ellen's escapade spread through Athens like wildfire, the town found itself split into two camps. The aisles of Kroger became the unofficial battleground for heated debates about Ellen's sanity and heroism.

"I always knew that woman was a few cards short of a full deck," Mrs. Henderson sniffed as she inspected a cantaloupe. "Remember when she tried to convince the city council to replace all the Historic District Paint regulations? Crazy as a loon, I tell you."

"Now hold on just a minute," Mr. Johnson interjected, abandoning his search for the perfect Tomato. "Ellen may be... unconventional, but what she did was downright heroic!"

The produce section erupted into a chorus of conflicting opinions.

"She's always been odd, but this takes the cake."

"I heard she's been talking to squirrels in her backyard for years."

"Well, I think she's a saint. Not all heroes wear capes, you know!"

As the town continued to buzz with speculation and debate, one thing became clear: Athens would never be the same again. And in the end, whether saint or lunatic, Ellen had accomplished something remarkable – she had united the town in its fascination with her tale.

Act 3. The Ponderance: From Whispers to Legends

On one hand, gossip serves as a social lubricant, smoothing the gears of human interaction. It's the whispered secrets at the water cooler, the hushed conversations at family gatherings, the excited chatter among friends. In these moments, gossip creates intimacy, fostering a sense of trust and belonging among those sharing the information.

Evolutionary psychologists argue that gossip played a crucial role in our species' survival. As human societies grew larger and more complex, gossip became an efficient way to transmit important social information. Who can be trusted? Who's breaking the rules? This knowledge, spread through gossip, helped our ancestors navigate their social world and cooperate effectively in large groups.

Even today, studies show that gossip can have prosocial effects. It can warn group members about untrustworthy individuals, enforce social norms, and even reduce stress. In this light, gossip appears as a fundamental aspect of human nature, a tool for social bonding and community building.

Yet, on the other hand, gossip can be a weapon of destruction. The same whispers that bring some together can ostracize others. Reputations built over years can be shattered by a single rumor. The line between harmless chatter and malicious slander is often blurry, and once crossed, the damage can be irreparable.

In the age of social media, the potential for gossip to cause harm has been amplified exponentially. What once might have been a localized rumor can now spread globally in a matter of hours. The anonymity provided by digital platforms often removes the social checks that might have restrained more malicious forms of gossip in face-to-face interactions.

Moreover, the addictive nature of salacious information can lead to a culture of constant judgment and scrutiny. This environment can stifle creativity, breed paranoia, and erode trust within communities.

Between these two extremes lies a vast gray area where most gossip occurs. It's the curious mix of truth and speculation, of genuine concern and idle curiosity. It's the human attempt to understand our social world, to make sense of the behaviors and motivations of those around us.

This is where gossip intersects with storytelling, where today's rumor might become tomorrow's legend. Just as our ancestors gathered around fires to share tales of heroes and villains, we gather in our modern spaces – both physical and digital – to weave narratives about the people in our lives.

Understanding the dual nature of gossip is crucial to navigating our social landscape. It challenges us to be mindful of the information and how we share it. Can we harness the connecting power of gossip while minimizing its potential for harm? Can we satisfy our natural curiosity about others without infringing on their privacy?

As the sun sets on our tale of Ellen Beaumont and the whispers that swept through Athens, Georgia, we're left to ponder the power of stories and the complex web of human connection they weave.

In the end, Ellen's ordeal was born not from a real threat, but from the perfect storm of fear, love, and misinformation. Her story, now etched into the collective memory of Athens, serves as a poignant reminder of how easily our deepest fears can be manipulated and how the lines between reality and perception can blur in the face of perceived danger.

But let us not judge Ellen too harshly. In her misguided actions, we see a reflection of our own vulnerabilities, our own capacity for both love and folly. Her tale, whispered over Seven and Sevens in local bars, shared in hushed tones at the grocery store, and debated in living rooms across town, has become more than just a cautionary tale. It has become a part of Athens itself, another thread in the rich tapestry of stories that bind this community together.

As we reflect on the nature of gossip and its role in our lives, we're reminded that every rumor, every whispered secret, carries with it the potential for both harm and healing. Like the perfect blend of whiskey and soda in a Seven and Seven, the art of storytelling requires balance—a mix of truth and speculation, of empathy and curiosity.

In the end, perhaps that's what the whispers of Athens teach us. In our stories, be they gossip, legend, or lived experience, we find our shared humanity. They remind us of our capacity for love, our susceptibility to fear, and our enduring need for connection.

So the next time you hear a whisper, a piece of juicy gossip, or an unbelievable tale, pause for a moment. Consider the story behind the story—the very human desires and fears that drive us to share, to speculate, to connect. And remember Ellen Beaumont, whose love for her son echoed through the streets of Athens, reminding us all of the power of a mother's love, the dangers of unchecked fear, and the enduring strength of community.

In Athens, Georgia, as in small towns and big cities across the world, it is our stories that bind us, our whispers that connect us, and our shared experiences—both tragic and triumphant—that make us who we are.

And so, as the cicadas buzz their evening song and porch lights flicker on across Athens, another day fades into memory. But the whispers? The whispers live on, carried on by the warm Southern breeze, waiting for the next eager ear, the next storyteller, and the next chapter in the ever-unfolding story of our shared human experience.

9

THE MIRROR'S REFLECTION

Act 1. The Spirits: Old Fashioned

As the eerie tale of Larry and the mysterious mirror unfolds, one can't help but feel a chill run down their spine. In moments like these, when the line between reality and the supernatural blurs, there's comfort to be found in the familiar rituals of everyday life. Perhaps it's in the act of creating something tangible, something that engages all the senses, that we can ground ourselves in the present moment. What better way to do this than by crafting a classic cocktail—an Old Fashioned? This timeless drink, with its rich history and complex flavors, serves as an anchor to reality, a reminder of the simple pleasures that exist beyond the realm of the uncanny.

As the evening deepens and the world outside your window grows quieter, you find yourself drawn to create a cocktail that embodies timeless sophistication. Your mind settles on the perfect choice: an Old Fashioned, a drink as classic as they come.

You begin by selecting a heavy-bottomed rock glass. Its

solid weight in your hand feels reassuring, promising to cradle your creation perfectly. You place a large ice cube in the glass, its clear surface gleaming in the soft light of your study.

First comes the foundation of sweetness. You reach for a sugar cube and place it at the bottom of the glass. With a dropper, you add a few dashes of Angostura bitters, watching as the dark liquid seeps into the sugar, creating a small pool of amber at the base.

Next, you pour in a small splash of water. With a muddler, you gently crush the sugar cube, working it into a paste with the bitters and water. The aroma of spices rises, hinting at the complexity to come.

Now for the star of the show—the whiskey. You select a bottle of premium bourbon or rye, whose rich amber color promises depth and warmth. As you uncap it, the scent of oak and vanilla fills the air. You pour two ounces over the muddled sugar and bitters, watching as it swirls and mingles with the spices.

With a bar spoon, you gently stir the mixture. The ice cube clinks softly against the glass as you rotate the spoon, chilling the drink and allowing the flavors to meld. You continue for about 30 seconds, until the glass outside frosts slightly over.

For the finishing touch, you reach for an orange. With a sharp knife, you cut a swath of peel, making sure to avoid the bitter white pith. You hold the peel over the glass, with the outer side down, and give it a firm twist. A fine mist of aromatic oils sprays over the surface of the drink, adding a bright, citrusy note to the mix. Before dropping it into the drink, you run the peel around the glass rim.

As a final flourish, you spear a cocktail cherry with a

pick and gently place it in the glass; its deep red color is a striking contrast to the amber liquid.

You step back to admire your handiwork. The Old Fashioned stands before you, a visual testament to the art of cocktail making. The large ice cube keeps the drink perfectly chilled without over-diluting, while the orange peel and cherry add pops of color to the rich, amber liquid.

As you lift the glass to your lips, the aroma hits you first —a complex bouquet of whiskey, spices, and citrus. The first sip is a revelation. The whiskey provides a robust, warming base, while the sugar and bitters create a perfect balance of sweet and bitter. The orange oils add a bright top note, and the slow-melting ice cube ensures that each sip is as perfectly balanced as the last.

In this moment, you realize you've created more than just a cocktail. This Old Fashioned is a sensory journey, a perfect encapsulation of the art of mixology. It's a reminder of why this drink has stood the test of time, delighting palates for over a century.

As you settle into your favorite leather armchair, Old Fashioned in hand, you can't help but feel a connection to the long lineage of cocktail enthusiasts who have enjoyed this very same drink. With each sip, you savor not just the flavors but also the history and craftsmanship perfectly distilled into this timeless classic. The ice clinks gently against the glass as you raise it in a silent toast to the perfect end of the day, captured in the amber depths of your beautifully crafted Old Fashioned.

As you sip your perfectly crafted Old Fashioned, let the warmth of the whiskey and the complex interplay of flavors remind you of the solid, dependable aspects of your world. Unlike the shifting reflections in Larry's mysterious mirror, this drink is a constant, a touchstone of reality. It's a creation you can see, smell, taste, and feel - a sensory experience that affirms your presence in the here and now. As the ice slowly melts and the flavors evolve, take a moment to reflect on the story you've just encountered. Perhaps, like the Old Fashioned, the best approach to life's mysteries is to savor them slowly, appreciating their complexity without allowing them to overwhelm us. After all, in a world where the line between the ordinary and the extraordinary can blur in an instant, sometimes the most comforting thing we can do is to raise a glass to the unknown and take another sip of the familiar.

You know, there's something magical about being a wayfaring stranger in this vast world of ours. As I ramble from place to place, I've found that the most interesting people cross my path, each carrying a story as unique as their fingerprints. Today's tale is one such gem, plucked from the crossroads of chance and mystery.

A few years ago, I met a new friend – let's call him Larry. Our paths crossed in Augusta, Georgia, where the old South whispers secrets to those willing to listen. Larry shared with me a story that sent shivers down my spine—a tale of an antique mirror and the strange occurrences that followed its arrival in his life.

Now, mirrors have long held a special place in our folklore. From Snow White's stepmother's "Mirror, mirror on the wall" to the superstitions about breaking them, these reflective surfaces have always been more than mere objects. They're portals, truth-tellers, and sometimes, harbingers of the uncanny.

But Larry's story reminds us of something crucial: we must be careful about what we bring into our personal spaces. Every object carries its own energy and its own history. And sometimes, these additions to our environment can change how we see ourselves – quite literally, in this case.

So, as we dive into Larry's eerie experience, I invite you to reflect – pun intended – on the power of the objects that surround us. How do they shape our perceptions? Our realities? And what happens when the line between the familiar and the fantastical begins to blur?

Settle in, fellow travelers. The night is young, and the story that awaits us might just change the way you look at your own reflection. Welcome to "The Mirror's Gaze" – a tale of art, antiquity, and the shadows that lurk just beyond the glass.

Act 2. The Tale: The Mirror's Reflection

Larry Thornton stood back from the wall, paintbrush in hand, admiring his latest creation. The mural, a vibrant depiction of Augusta's Riverwalk at sunset, was nearly complete. He'd been working on it for weeks, transforming the bland office lobby of Riverside Graphics into a captivating scene that seemed to glow with an inner light.

As he dabbed a touch more orange onto a cloud, reflecting the last rays of the painted sun, a voice startled him from behind.

"It's beautiful, Larry. You've really outdone yourself this time."

Larry turned to see Margaret, the company's owner, standing in the doorway. Her silver hair was neatly coiffed, and her eyes sparkled with appreciation as she gazed at the mural.

"Thanks, Margaret," Larry replied, wiping his hands on his paint-spattered jeans. "I think it's coming along nicely. Should be finished by the end of the week."

Margaret nodded, then seemed to remember something. "Oh! I almost forgot. I have something for you." She disappeared for a moment, then returned carrying a large, flat object wrapped in brown paper.

Larry set down his brush and palette; his curiosity piqued. "What's this?"

"A little token of appreciation," Margaret said, handing him the package. "For all your hard work, not just on this mural, but everything you've done for the company over the years."

Carefully, Larry unwrapped the gift. As the paper fell away, he found himself staring at an ornate, antique mirror. The frame was silver, tarnished with age, and adorned with intricate floral designs and what appeared to be faces worked into the metalwork. The glass itself was slightly cloudy, giving it a dreamlike quality.

"Wow," Larry breathed, genuinely impressed. "This is... something else. Where did you find it?"

Margaret's smile faltered for just a moment, so briefly that Larry thought he might have imagined it. "Oh, it's been in my family for generations. I've always loved it, but I thought it would suit your apartment perfectly. That beautiful old building you live in... this mirror belongs in a place with history."

Larry ran his fingers along the frame, tracing the delicate patterns. "It's incredible. Thank you, Margaret. I'll hang it as soon as I get home."

As Larry carefully wrapped the mirror back up, he didn't notice the way Margaret's eyes lingered on it, a mixture of relief and something that might have been regret flickering across her face.

Later that evening, Larry lugged the mirror up the creaking stairs of his apartment building. The structure, once the home of a prominent banker who built it in the 1850s, had been converted into apartments in the 1970s. Larry's unit, on the third floor, still retained much of its original charm – high ceilings, ornate moldings, and large windows that overlooked Greene Street.

He found the perfect spot for the mirror: on a bare wall in his bedroom, opposite his bed. As he hung it, he couldn't shake the feeling that the cloudy glass was watching him. Shaking off the ridiculous notion, Larry stepped back to admire the effect.

The mirror did indeed suit the room perfectly. Its tarnished silver frame complemented the faded grandeur of the apartment, and even in the dim light of his bedside lamp, it seemed to capture and amplify what little illumination there was.

"Well," Larry said to his reflection, "welcome home."

As he turned away to get ready for bed, he could have sworn he saw something move in the mirror's depths. But when he looked back, there was nothing but his own tired face staring back at him.

That night, Larry dreamed of corridors that stretched endlessly, doors that opened onto impossible rooms, and always, just at the edge of his vision, a flicker of movement that vanished when he turned to look.

He awoke with a start, heart pounding, to find his room bathed in silvery moonlight. The mirror gleamed in the darkness, and for a moment, Larry could have sworn he saw a face that wasn't his own gazing back at him.

But then he blinked, and it was gone.

The next few days passed uneventfully for Larry. He finished the mural at Riverside Graphics, earning effusive praise from Margaret and the rest of the staff. Yet despite his professional success, he found himself increasingly distracted by thoughts of the mirror.

It wasn't that anything particularly strange had happened. The mirror hung on his bedroom wall, innocuous and silent. But Larry couldn't shake the feeling that something had changed in his apartment since its arrival.

On Friday night, after a long week of work, Larry decided to unwind with a glass of wine and some sketching. He sat at his drafting table in the living room, soft jazz playing in the background, as he worked on ideas for his next personal project – a series of paintings inspired by Augusta's haunted history.

As the hour grew late, Larry felt his eyelids growing heavy. He set down his pencil and stretched, deciding it was time for bed. But as he walked towards his bedroom, he froze.

While he was there, he heard something in the hallway. A whisper, so faint he almost thought he'd imagined it. Larry held his breath, straining to listen.

"...Larry..."

It was barely audible, like the rustle of leaves in a gentle breeze. However, it was there, and it clearly stated his name.

Heart pounding, Larry flicked on the hallway light. Nothing. Just the familiar sight of his framed artwork on the walls and the worn hardwood floor beneath his feet.

"Get a grip, Thornton," he muttered to himself. "You're letting your imagination run wild."

Still, as he prepared for bed, Larry couldn't quite shake his unease. He found himself avoiding looking directly at the mirror as he changed into his pajamas, an irrational fear gripping him that he might see something – or someone – looking back.

As he lay in bed, staring at the ceiling, Larry's mind wandered to the mirror's history. Margaret had said it had been in her family for generations, but she hadn't offered any specifics. Perhaps, he thought, learning more about its provenance might put his mind at ease.

Eventually, Larry drifted into an uneasy sleep. His dreams were fragmented and strange, full of shadowy figures and echoing laughter. He tossed and turned, tangling himself in his sheets.

In the depths of the night, Larry's eyes snapped open. He lay perfectly still, every muscle tense. Something had woken him, but he wasn't sure what.

Then he heard it. Footsteps. Slow, deliberate footsteps moved across the floor of his bedroom.

But that was impossible. He lived alone, and he always locked his door.

Larry's breath caught in his throat as the footsteps drew nearer to his bed. He wanted to turn to confront whatever was in his room, but fear held him paralyzed.

The footsteps stopped right beside his bed. Larry could feel a presence looming over him; he could almost sense eyes boring into the back of his head.

Summoning every ounce of courage he possessed, Larry rolled over.

Nothing. The room was empty.

But as his racing heart began to slow, Larry's eyes were drawn to the mirror. In the dim light filtering through his curtains, he could have sworn he saw a figure retreating into its depths, like a person walking away down a long corridor.

Larry blinked, and the image was gone. Just his own wide-eyed reflection stared back at him.

Sleep did not come easily for the rest of the night.

The next morning, as Larry was nursing a strong cup of

coffee, his phone rang. It was his downstairs neighbor, Mrs. Abernathy, an elderly woman who'd lived in the building for decades.

"Larry, dear," she said, her voice filled with concern, "is everything alright up there?"

"Yes, Mrs. Abernathy," Larry replied, stifling a yawn. "Why do you ask?"

"Well, there was quite a commotion last night. There was a lot of thumping and moving around. I was worried you might have taken ill or something."

Larry felt a chill run down his spine. "What time was this, Mrs. Abernathy?"

"Oh, must have been around 3 AM. Woke me right up, it did."

After assuring Mrs. Abernathy that he was fine and apologizing for the disturbance – though he had no idea what could have caused it – Larry hung up the phone. He stared at the coffee mug in his hands, watching the dark liquid tremble as his hands shook slightly.

Larry spent the rest of the weekend in a state of nervous agitation. He found himself avoiding his bedroom, choosing instead to nap fitfully on the couch. Every creak of the old building made him jump, and he couldn't shake the feeling of being watched.

On Monday morning, Larry arrived at work looking haggard. Dark circles underlined his eyes, and his usually neat appearance was disheveled. Margaret noticed immediately.

"Larry, are you feeling alright?" she asked, concern evident in her voice.

He forced a smile. "Just a bit under the weather. Nothing to worry about."

But as he worked on a new design project, Larry found

his mind wandering back to the mirror. He opened a web browser and began researching antique mirrors, hoping to find something similar to the one Margaret had given him.

Hours slipped by as Larry fell down a rabbit hole of folklore and superstition surrounding mirrors. He read about their use in divination, their supposed ability to trap souls, and countless ghost stories featuring mysterious reflective surfaces.

One particular legend caught his attention: a tale of a cursed mirror that showed glimpses of other times and places, slowly driving its owners mad. In the story, the description of the mirror was eerily similar to the one hanging in his bedroom.

Larry shook his head, trying to dispel the ridiculous thoughts. It was just an old mirror, nothing more. Yet he couldn't quite convince himself of that.

As he was packing up to leave for the day, Margaret appeared at his desk again.

"Larry, I couldn't help but notice... that mirror I gave you. How do you like it?"

There was something in her tone that made Larry pause. "It's... interesting," he said carefully. "I was actually wondering if you could tell me more about its history."

Margaret's smile faltered for a moment. "Oh, you know how these old family heirlooms are. Stories get muddled over time. I'm afraid I don't know much more than what I told you."

Before Larry could press further, Margaret made an excuse about a meeting and hurried away, leaving him with more questions than answers.

That night, Larry stood before the mirror, studying it intently. The faces that worked into the frame appeared to leer at him, their expressions shifting subtly in the dim light.

He reached out to touch the glass, half-expecting his hand to pass through it like water.

Instead, his fingers met a cold, solid surface. But as he pulled his hand away, he could have sworn he saw finger-prints remaining on the glass – fingerprints that weren't his own.

Larry stumbled back, his heart racing. He blinked hard, and when he looked again, the mirror was clear. Just his own pale, frightened face stared back at him.

Sleep eluded him that night. Larry tossed and turned, plagued by half-formed nightmares. In his dreams, he wandered endless corridors lined with mirrors, each one showing a different scene at a different time. And as always, just at the edge of his vision, a shadowy figure watched and waited.

He awoke with a start, drenched in sweat. The bedroom was bathed in an eerie, silvery light. Larry's eyes were drawn inexorably to the mirror.

What he saw made his blood run cold.

Instead of his bedroom's reflection, the mirror showed a grand, old-fashioned parlor. Candlelight flickered, illuminating heavy velvet drapes and ornate furniture. And there, in the center of the room, stood a woman in a high-collared Victorian dress, her back to Larry.

Slowly and terribly, the woman began to turn.

Larry scrambled out of bed, stumbling out of the bedroom and slamming the door behind him. He spent the rest of the night huddled on the couch, jumping at every sound.

The next few days passed in a blur of paranoia and exhaustion. Larry's work began to suffer; he missed deadlines and made careless mistakes. His colleagues whispered concerns about his erratic behavior and disheveled appearance.

At home, the strange occurrences intensified. Objects would move when Larry wasn't looking. He'd hear whispers and footsteps when he was alone in the apartment. And always, always, he felt watched.

The mirror became the center of his obsession. Larry spent hours staring into its depths, convinced he could see movement and flashes of other places and times. Sometimes, he thought he glimpsed faces – not his own, but others—gaunt and pleading.

One night, driven to the brink of madness by a lack of sleep and constant fear, Larry made a decision. The mirror had to go.

He wrapped it carefully in blankets, struggling with its unexpected weight. As he maneuvered it through his apartment, he could have sworn he heard muffled screams coming from within the swaddled bundle.

Larry staggered down the stairs, his mirror becoming heavier with each step. Finally, he reached the alley behind the building. With a grunt of effort, he propped the mirror against the wall, next to the dumpster.

As he turned to leave, a flicker of movement caught his eye. Larry looked back.

The blanket had fallen away, revealing the mirror's surface. But instead of the dirty alley, Larry saw his own bedroom reflected in the glass. And there, standing in the center of the room, was a figure.

It was Larry himself, but not as he is now. This version of him was gaunt, wild-eyed, and his hair shot through with gray. The other Larry pressed his hands against the glass, his mouth opening in a silent scream.

Real Larry stumbled back, his heart pounding. He

turned and ran, not stopping until he was back in his apartment, the door locked behind him.

The next morning, Larry awoke on his couch, groggy and disoriented. Had it all been a nightmare? Cautiously, he made his way to the bedroom.

The mirror was gone.

Relief washed over him, followed quickly by doubt. He hurried downstairs and out into the alley.

There was no sign of the mirror.

In the days that followed, Larry's life slowly returned to normal. His sleep improved, his work recovered, and the oppressive feeling of being watched gradually faded.

But sometimes, late at night, he would wake with a start, convinced he'd heard whispers or footsteps. And in those moments, Larry couldn't shake the feeling that somewhere, in some other time or place, another version of himself was still trapped, staring out from behind the clouded glass of an antique mirror.

As for Margaret, she never mentioned the mirror again. But sometimes, when she thought Larry wasn't looking, he would catch her watching him with an expression of mingled relief and guilt.

And in the alley behind the apartment building, if one looked closely, they might notice a faint, silvery rectangle on the wall where the mirror had briefly rested – a ghostly reminder of the thin barrier between our world and whatever lies beyond the looking glass.

Act 3. The Ponderance: Be careful what you bring into your home, as it may change how you reflect on things

Antoine de Saint-Exupéry's profound statement, "What is essential is invisible to the eye," from *The Little Prince*, invites us to look beyond the surface and consider the intangible aspects of life. This philosophy emphasizes the importance of emotions, relationships, and values that cannot be seen but profoundly impact our existence. In contrast, there's a growing awareness of how our physical and digital environments, both visible and invisible, shape our thoughts, emotions, and behaviors.

As we come to the end of Larry's unsettling tale, we find ourselves peering into the depths of our own reflections, both literal and metaphorical. The story of the haunted mirror serves as a powerful reminder of the unseen forces that shape our perception of reality.

Just as Larry's antique mirror seemed to blur the lines between the tangible and the intangible, we too often find ourselves navigating the hazy boundaries between what we can see and what we can only sense. The objects we surround ourselves with, the spaces we inhabit, and the digital realms we frequent all contribute to the invisible tapestry of our daily lives.

In a world where the visible and invisible constantly intertwine, perhaps the wisest course is to approach life with the same care and intentionality as crafting the perfect Old Fashioned. We must select our experiences and surroundings with discernment, blend them thoughtfully, and take the time to savor the complex flavors they create.

As you reflect on Larry's experience, consider the mirrors in your own life - not just the physical ones, but the metaphorical reflections that shape your perception of self and reality. What do they reveal? What might they conceal? And most importantly, how do they influence the story you're writing with your life?

Remember, like the Old Fashioned cocktail we began with, life is a careful balance of elements—the sweet, the bitter, the strong, and the subtle. It's up to us to find harmony among them, always mindful that what we bring into our lives has the power to transform us in ways both seen and unseen.

So, the next time you catch your reflection in a mirror, take a moment to look beyond the surface. You might just discover that the most intriguing stories are the ones that exist in the spaces between reality and imagination, in the reflections that go deeper than what the eye can see.

10

THE SAYRE HOUSE

Act 1. The Spirits: Crown and Ginger

As the tale of the Sayre House unfolds, with its secrets and whispered histories, one can't help but crave a drink that embodies both comfort and intrigue. Enter the Crown and Ginger, a cocktail that, like the house itself, blends the familiar with the unexpected. Just as Robert found solace in Sparta's grand rooms, so too can we find respite in this classic combination. Let's craft a drink that will ease the tensions on a fateful night.

As the evening settles in, a crisp autumn breeze rustles through the leaves outside your window. You find yourself craving something warm and spicy, yet refreshing. In an instant, the answer comes to you: a crown and ginger.

You begin by selecting a tall, elegant highball glass from your collection. Its sleek shape promises to perfectly showcase your creation's golden hues. You fill it generously with ice, the cubes clinking musically against the glass, setting the stage for what's to come.

Next, you reach for the bottle of Crown Royal, its purple

velvet bag a tactile reminder of the whisky's regal heritage. As you remove the bottle, the light catches on its faceted surface, hinting at the complexity within. You pour a generous double shot over the ice, watching as the amber liquid weaves its way through the cracks, releasing subtle notes of vanilla and oak.

Now for the ginger ale - the crown's effervescent dance partner. You select a premium brand known for its robust ginger flavor. As you crack open the can or twist off the bottle cap, a spicy aroma fills the air, mingling enticingly with the whisky's warmth. Slowly, you pour the ginger ale over the Crown Royal and ice, admiring how it froths and bubbles, creating a perfect golden sunset in your glass.

The ratio is crucial here; you aim for one part Crown to three parts ginger ale, but adjust to your liking. As the drink comes together, you observe how the colors blend, creating a rich, inviting hue that seems to glow from within.

For a finishing touch, you decide to add a twist. You reach for a fresh lime, its green skin bright against your cutting board. With a sharp knife, you cut a wheel of lime, releasing a burst of citrus into the air. You run the lime around the rim of the glass before gently dropping it into the drink, adding a hint of tartness to balance the sweet and spicy notes.

You step back to admire your handiwork. The Crown and Ginger stand before you, a perfect blend of sophistication and comfort. Condensation begins to form on the outside of the glass, promising a cool, invigorating sip.

As you lift the drink to your lips, the aroma hits you first: a harmonious blend of smooth whisky, spicy ginger, and bright citrus. The first sip is a revelation. The warmth of the Crown Royal is perfectly tempered by the crisp, bubbly ginger ale. The lime adds just the right touch of brightness, elevating the entire experience.

In this moment, you realize you've created more than just a cocktail. This Crown and Ginger is a sensory journey —a perfect balance of flavors and textures. It's a reminder that sometimes, the most satisfying combinations are those that bring together the familiar in new, exciting ways.

As you settle into your favorite armchair, drink in hand, you can't help but feel a sense of contentment. This Crown and Ginger isn't just a drink - it's a companion for a cozy evening, a toast to the simple pleasures of life. With each sip, you savor not just the flavors but the moment itself, perfectly captured in a glass.

As you sip your crown and ginger, let it transport you to Sayre House on that pivotal night. Each taste is a reminder of the complexities of life, love, and the choices we make. Like Robert and Michael's unexpected connection, this cocktail brings together elements that shouldn't work, yet somehow create something beautiful. It's a drink for story-tellers and dreamers, for those who seek adventure. So raise your glass to the tales yet untold, to the secrets of small towns, and to the power of a well-mixed drink to bring people together, even in the most unlikely of circumstances.

Picture this: a grand Greek Revival mansion, its columns standing proud against the Georgia sky, but its windows shuttered and its rooms silent for decades. This is the Sayre House, a once-magnificent home in the small town of Sparta, Georgia, that became an unexpected inheritance for the Georgia Trust for Historic Preservation.

But the story of how this house came into the Trust's possession is where our tale really begins. As I stood on the creaking floorboards of this long-abandoned home, piecing together fragments of local lore and whispering rumors, a narrative emerged that was complex and captivating.

It's a story that spans generations, from a librarian's final bequest to her son's tragic demise at the foot of a grand ole grand staircase. The house had remained untouched since that fateful day, as if frozen in time. Local gossip painted a colorful picture of the son – a charismatic figure who allegedly dabbled in cocaine smuggling during the heady days of the 1990s. According to reports, someone found him dead at the newel post. He left behind a place that felt almost haunted by him.

As I worked inside the house, collecting these tidbits from the locals, I found myself drawn to the story of the life of this enigmatic man. In a small Southern town, his lifestyle must have set him apart, perhaps isolating him in ways that went beyond his illicit activities. It made me wonder about the challenges he might have faced and the secrets he might have kept.

This is a tale of fortunes made and lost, of a life lived on the edge, and of a house that stands as a silent witness to it all. But more than that, it's a story I felt compelled to tell – and perhaps, in some small way, to rewrite. In crafting this narrative, I found myself wanting to imagine a different ending for the owner of Sayre House.

It's a story that spans generations, from a librarian's final bequest to her son's untimely death, and even further back, to the cocaine-fueled excesses of the 1990s. It's a tale of secrets hidden behind Greek Revival facades, of fortunes made and lost.

Act 2. The Tale: The Sayre House

The night air hung thick and heavy as Robert pulled his Firebird Trans Am T-Top into the crowded lot behind Backstreet. The pulsing beat of electronic music throbbed through the walls, a siren song luring Atlanta's restless souls into its neon-lit embrace. It was July 27, 1996 - a night that would etch itself into the city's memory for reasons yet unknown.

Robert killed the engine, his eyes darting across the sea of vehicles. He reached into the passenger seat, fingers closing around the cool leather of his duffel bag, its contents a powder more precious than gold to the revelers inside.

As he approached the back entrance, Trey, one of the club's bouncers, nodded in silent recognition. The heavy metal door swung open, engulfing Robert in a cacophony of sound and swirling light.

On its three levels, Backstreet pulsed like a living organism, a labyrinth of pleasure and excess. Bodies writhed on the dance floor, a mass of sweat-slicked skin and glitter. In dark alcoves and bathroom stalls, furtive exchanges took place—chemical keys to unlocking inhibitions.

Robert made his way through the crowd, finding his contact in his usual spot—a private booth overlooking the main floor. Robert allowed himself a thin smile as he slid into a booth. The duffel bag disappeared beneath the table, replaced moments later by a thick envelope.

As Robert pocketed the envelope, a young man approached the booth. His glassy and unfocused eyes fixed on Robert with an intensity that was unsettling.

"My man!" Joey shouted over the din, pulling Robert into an embrace. "You're a lifesaver, you know that?

"You look like you could use a drink," the stranger sitting at the bar beside him said, his voice barely audible above the music. "How about a Crown and Ginger?"

Robert hesitated, years of caution warring with an unexpected curiosity. Against his better judgment, he nodded. "Lead the way," he said gruffly.

The stranger, who introduced himself as Michael, led Robert to the bar. They watched in silence as the bartender mixed their drinks, the amber liquid swirling hypnotically in the low light.

"To new friends," Michael said, raising his glass. Robert clinked his own against it, the familiar burn of whiskey warming his throat.

As they sipped their drinks, Robert found himself opening up. There was something about Michael's earnest face, his attentive gaze, that broke through Robert's carefully constructed walls.

"You want to really celebrate?" With a mischievous glint in his eye, Michael asked. He jerked his head towards the bathrooms, his meaning clear.

Robert knew he should refuse, stick to business, and leave. But the night felt charged with possibility, the air electric with unspoken promise. He nodded as he followed Michael through the crowd.

The bathroom was a stark contrast to the pulsing energy of the club; it was dark and barely lit, with graffiti-covered stalls. Michael produced a small bag of white powder; his movements were quick and practiced.

"You first," he offered, holding out a carefully measured line on the back of his hand.

Robert hesitated for only a moment before leaning in. The familiar rush hit him almost instantly, sharpening his senses and setting his nerves alight. He watched as Michael took his own hit, the young man's pupils dilating in the harsh light.

"Now," Michael said, grinning widely, "let's really enjoy this night."

They emerged from the bathroom to find the club in chaos. CNN was broadcast on the TVs throughout the club, with urgent voices rising above the muted music. "There's been a bombing," someone nearby said, their voice trembling.

Joie Chen of CNN was on the TV screen interviewing some San Francisco tourist who was taking video of a concert at the park where the bombing occurred

The news spread like wildfire, casting a pall over the revelry. Robert felt a chill run down his spine, his sudden sobriety crashing over him like a wave. They went back to the bathroom stall.

The bathroom stall at Backstreet felt like a world unto itself, removed from the pulsing chaos beyond its flimsy metal walls. Robert leaned against the graffiti-covered partition, watching as Michael carefully divided the white powder into two neat lines. The dim light cast shadows across the younger man's face, accentuating the sharp angles of his cheekbones and the intensity in his eyes.

"You know," Michael said, glancing up with a sly grin, "I've seen you around here before. Always wondered what your story was."

Robert raised an eyebrow, a mix of wariness and intrigue coloring his response. "Oh yeah? And what did you imagine?"

Michael straightened up, moving closer until Robert could feel the heat radiating off his body. "I imagined someone dangerous," he murmured, voice low and tinged with excitement. "Someone with secrets."

Their eyes locked, and Robert felt a jolt of electricity course through him. It had been a long time since anyone had looked at him like that – with a mixture of desire and genuine curiosity. He found himself leaning in, drawn by some magnetic pull he couldn't quite explain.

"Dangerous, huh?" Robert's voice was rougher than he intended. "Maybe you shouldn't be in here with me, then."

Michael's grin widened. "Maybe that's exactly where I want to be." He held out his hand with the carefully prepared line of cocaine balanced on its back. "Care to do the honors?"

Robert hesitated for only a moment before bending down. The familiar burn in his nostrils was followed almost immediately by a rush of euphoria. He watched as Michael took his own hit, transfixed by the way the younger man's head tilted back, exposing the long line of his throat.

As the drug took effect, the small space in the stall seemed to shrink even further. Robert was acutely aware of every point where their bodies nearly touched, as well as of the electricity that crackled in the scant inches between them.

"So," Michael said, his pupils dilated and a slight flush creeping up his neck, "what's your poison? Besides the obvious, I mean." He gestured vaguely at the remnants of powder on his hand.

The sound was low and gravelly, and Robert chuckled. "Crown and Ginger, usually. You offering to buy me a drink?"

"Might be," Michael replied, his fingers trailing lightly down Robert's arm. "If you're planning on sticking around for a while."

The touch sent shivers down Robert's spine, awakening feelings he'd long since buried. Part of him knew he should leave, should stick to business and maintain the careful distance he'd cultivated over years in this dangerous game. But the cocaine singing in his veins and the heat in Michael's eyes made rational thought increasingly difficult.

"I could be persuaded," Robert found himself saying, surprising even himself with the flirtatious tone that crept into his voice.

They emerged from the stall, the club's pounding music hitting them like a physical force after the relative silence of the bathroom. Michael's hand found the small of Robert's back, guiding him through the writhing crowd toward the bar. The casual intimacy of the gesture sent another jolt through Robert's system.

As they waited for their drinks, Michael leaned in close, his lips nearly brushing Robert's ear. "So, what's your story? Really? I'm guessing you're not just here for the music and ambiance."

Robert turned; their faces were now inches apart. "What makes you say that?"

Michael's eyes sparkled with mischief. "Let's just say I'm observant. The way you move, the way people react to you... you're not just another club kid looking for a good time."

"Maybe I'm undercover vice," Robert said, only half-joking.

Michael threw his head back and laughed, the sound rich and genuine. "Please. If you were a cop, I'd eat my shoes." His expression grew more serious, though the playful glint remained in his eyes. "No, you're something much more interesting."

Their drinks arrived, and they found a relatively quiet corner to continue their conversation. As they talked,

Robert found himself opening up more than he had in years. There was something disarming about Michael's earnest curiosity, the way he listened without judgment.

As the night wore on and the drinks kept flowing, Robert felt the walls he'd so carefully constructed begin to crumble. When news of the bombing at Centennial Olympic Park rippled through the club, he saw his own shock and fear reflected in Michael's eyes.

In that moment of shared vulnerability, Robert made a decision that would alter the course of both their lives.

"Come home with me," he said, the words tumbling out before he could stop them.

Michael's eyes widened in surprise. "What?"

Robert took a deep breath, committing to the idea. "I've got a place, about two hours from here. Old house, quiet. We could... we could go there, get away from all this for a while."

He watched as a range of emotions played across Michael's face – surprise, excitement, and a flicker of something that might have been fear. But then Michael's expression settled into a smile that was equal parts nervous and exhilarated.

"You know what?" Michael said, downing the last of his drink. "Why the hell not? Let's go."

As they made their way out of the club, Robert felt a mix of anticipation and trepidation. He was breaking every rule he'd set for himself, letting someone into his carefully guarded world. But as Michael's hand found his in the darkness of the parking lot, he couldn't bring himself to regret it.

The Firebird roared to life, and they peeled out onto the empty streets of Atlanta. As the city lights faded behind them, Robert felt a sense of possibility he hadn't experienced in years. He knew that whatever happened next would change everything.

"Where are we going?" he asked, voice small and uncertain.

"Sparta," Robert replied, eyes fixed on the road ahead. "I've got a place there. The Sayre House."

As the Firebird Trans Am T-Top roared along Georgia's back roads, the first true light of day began to break over the horizon. Robert's hands gripped the steering wheel tightly, his eyes darting between the winding road ahead and the rearview mirror, old habits dying hard even in this moment of unexpected connection.

Michael sat in the passenger seat, his head tilted back against the headrest, his eyes half-closed, but a small smile played on his lips. The wind whipped through the open T-top, tousling their hair and carrying with it the rich, earthy scent of Georgia pines and dew-damp fields.

"I've never seen this part of the state," Michael said, his voice barely audible over the rush of wind and the rumble of the engine. "It's beautiful."

Robert nodded, a rare smile softening his usually stern features. He reached over and fiddled with the radio dial, searching for a clear station. Suddenly, the opening chords of Tracy Chapman's "Give Me One Reason" filled the car, her soulful voice a perfect complement to the golden light now spilling across the landscape.

Michael's eyes opened fully, and he turned to Robert with a look of pleasant surprise. "Man, I love this song," he said, his fingers tapping out the rhythm on his knee.

Robert's smile widened as he focused on the road ahead. "Yeah, it's a good one. Been hearing it everywhere lately."

As Tracy Chapman's lyrics about love and second chances floated through the air, both men fell into a comfortable silence. Michael began to hum along softly, his deep voice harmonizing with Chapman's. Robert found himself relaxing further, one hand leaving the wheel to rest casually on Michael's leg. The Trans Am ate up the miles, carrying them deeper into the heart of Georgia, while the music and the moment bound them together in a way neither had expected.

Robert nodded, allowing himself to see the familiar landscape through fresh eyes. The rolling hills, dotted with farmhouses and grazing cattle, took on an ethereal quality in the soft morning light. Mist clung to the low-lying areas, creating the illusion that they were driving through clouds.

"Wait till you see Sparta," Robert found himself saying. "It's like stepping back in time."

As they crested a hill, the small town came into view. Sparta, with its population barely over a thousand, sprawled out before them – a patchwork of Victorian homes and Greek Revival mansions.

Robert slowed the car as they entered the town proper, the quiet streets in stark contrast to the pulsing energy of Backstreet just hours before. A few early risers were out and about – an elderly man walking a dog.

"Over there," Robert said, nodding towards an imposing structure that dominated the town square. "That's the courthouse. Locals call it 'Her Majesty'."

Michael leaned forward, taking in the grand Victorian building with its red brick facade and ornate clock tower. "I can see why," he murmured. "It looks like something out of a fairy tale."

Robert chuckled. "Built in 1883. According to the story, the design aimed to resemble a French chateau.

"And that," he said, gesturing to a stately white building set back from the street, "is the Sparta Inn. Been there since the early 1800s."

Michael's eyes widened. "No way. It's still operating?"

Robert nodded. "On and off over the years. But its claim to fame is a party they threw for General Lafayette back in 1825."

"The Revolutionary War hero?" Michael asked, clearly impressed.

"The very same. He was doing a tour of the country, and Sparta pulled out all the stops. They say the party lasted all night, with dancing and toasts and all sorts of pomp and circumstance."

As they drove past, Robert could almost imagine the scene – ladies in flowing gowns, gentlemen in their finest attire, the sound of music and laughter spilling out into the night. It was a far cry from the quiet, slightly faded grandeur of the present-day inn, but there was still an undeniable air of history about the place.

"It's like a whole different world," Michael said softly, his eyes taking in every detail of the town. "How did you end up here, of all places?"

Robert was silent for a long moment, considering his answer. "Sometimes," he said finally, "the best place to hide is somewhere that feels like it's frozen in time. People here, they don't ask too many questions. They're happy to let you keep your secrets, as long as you respect theirs."

Michael turned to look at him, his expression a mixture of curiosity and concern. "And is that what you want? To keep hiding?"

The question hung in the air between them as Robert guided the car down Broad Street, where Sayre House stood waiting. Sayre House was nearly identical to the other Antebellum home located next door. He thought about the life he'd built here – the careful balance of secrecy and influence, the constant vigilance, the loneliness he'd convinced himself was a necessary sacrifice.

Then he glanced at Michael, this unexpected variable who'd thrown everything into question. For the first time in years, Robert found himself imagining a different kind of future – one where Sparta wasn't just a hiding place, but a home.

"I don't know," he admitted finally, his voice barely above a whisper. "I guess that's something I need to figure out."

"Welcome to Sparta," he said, managing a small smile. "For better or worse, this is my world."

Michael reached over, his hand covering Robert's where it still rested on the gear shift. "Thank you," he said simply. "For sharing it with me."

The Sayre House loomed before them, Casting long shadows across the overgrown hedges surrounding the house. This was his sanctuary, his fortress against the chaos of the world beyond.

Robert led Michael through the front door of Sayre House, the old hinges creaking in protest. As they stepped inside, the musty scent of old wood and fresh paint mingled in the air. Michael's eyes widened as he took in the grand central hall, its high ceilings and intricate moldings a testament to the home's former glory.

"Watch your step," Robert warned, gesturing to the canvas drop cloths that covered portions of the hardwood floor.

They moved deeper into the house, navigating around a rickety scaffold that stood sentry in the foyer. Michael's hand trailed along the banister of the sweeping staircase, his fingers coming away with a fine layer of sawdust. He led Michael into what was clearly intended to be the living room. A battered leather couch, incongruously modern among the vintage surroundings, faced a fireplace with its original marble mantle. Nearby, a bulky tube TV sat atop a milk crate, a VCR and a small collection of tapes scattered around it. "It's not much," Robert admitted, "but it's home."

Michael nodded, taking it all in. His gaze fell on a collection of tools and a toolbox in the corner, next to a half-finished bookshelf. Despite the chaos of renovation, there was something undeniably charming about the space – a sense of potential, of a work in progress. Just like their unexpected connection, Michael thought, as he turned to face Robert in the soft, dusty light of the old house.

He moved to an old stereo system tucked in the corner, fiddling with dials until the opening notes of George Michael's "Freedom" filled the room. The incongruity of the upbeat pop song in the cavernous, half-empty space wasn't lost on either of them.

"Dance with me," Robert said suddenly, holding out his hand.

Michael hesitated for only a moment before setting down his drink and stepping into Robert's arms. In the pre-dawn light, they swayed together, bodies close. As George Michael's voice soared through the chorus, Robert found himself singing along under his breath.

"I won't let you down, I will not give you up," he murmured, his lips close to Michael's ear.

Michael pulled back slightly, searching Robert's face. "Is that a promise?"

Act 3: We'll take' a cup o' kindness yet, for auld lang syne.

The mist rolled gently over the Northwest Georgia Mountains as I sat in my writing nook in Priscilla, My Camper, with my latest story manuscript spread before me. Little did

I know that the phone call I was about to make would be the last time I'd hear my friend Wayne's voice.

With a deep breath, I dialed his number in Fort Lauderdale, Florida. As the phone rang, I felt a mixture of anticipation and nervousness. I had never set foot in the fabled Backstreet, and yet I had dared to write about it, relying on whispered legends and secondhand tales.

"Hello?" Wayne's voice crackled through the line, warm despite the miles between us.

"Hey, Wayne," I said, "I've got something I want to read to you. It's a story... about Backstreet."

There was a pause, then a chuckle. "Backstreet? But you never—"

"I know," I interrupted gently. "But I've heard so many stories. Your stories. I wanted to try and capture it. Will you listen?"

As I began to read, the misty mountain air around me seemed to transform. I could hear Wayne's breathing, the occasional sharp intake of breath, the low murmurs of recognition. Though separated by hundreds of miles, we were transported together to the pulsing heart of 1990s Atlanta.

"It's like you were there," Wayne said when I finished, his voice thick with emotion. "The way you described the music, the energy... it's exactly how it felt." There was a wistfulness in his tone that tugged at my heart.

"Tell me more," I urged, pen poised over a notebook. "What else do you remember?"

And so, as the afternoon stretched into evening, Wayne's memories flowed across the miles. He spoke of a city electrified by the 1996 Olympics, of joy so palpable it seemed to hum in the air. I scribbled furiously, trying to capture every detail.

"You know," Wayne said, laughing, "I remember one night during the Olympics. My apartment was full of friends, and everyone was buzzing with excitement. My dog got so caught up in it all, she jumped right onto the coffee table, sent everyone's drinks flying. But no one cared. We were too happy, too caught up in the moment."

I smiled, imagining the scene. "The entire city was electrified with positive joy and energy," I repeated, a phrase Wayne had used earlier.

"Exactly," he said softly. "You've really captured that feeling in your story. You know, looking back, those were some of the happiest days of my life."

The distance between North Georgia and Fort Lauderdale seemed to shrink, bridged by shared stories and the power of memory.

With the discussion of parties and fun times almost without realizing it...in a tone of celebratory humor, I found myself humming the opening notes of "Auld Lang Syne." Its melody seemed to perfectly capture the happy emotions of our conversation.

"Should auld acquaintance be forgot, and never brought to mind?" I sang softly into the phone.

Wayne's voice joined mine, slightly off-key but filled with feeling. "We'll tak' a cup o' kindness yet, for auld lang syne."

As our impromptu duet faded, it now just seems right as a thought towards an ending... To keep these stories alive and to honor the vibrancy of a time I had never known firsthand but had come to cherish through the eyes of a friend,.

We said our goodbyes, neither of us knowing it would be our last conversation. A day or two later, Wayne would pass peacefully in his sleep, leaving behind a legacy of joy, friendship, and unforgettable memories. The spirit of those transformative times – the joy, the unity, and the sense of limitless possibility – continues to inspire and shape our understanding of the past. And though Wayne is no longer here to share more stories, his memories live on, a testament to the enduring power of friendship and the magic of a city in its most vibrant hour.

EPILOGUE

Closing Time: Savoring the Last Drop

As we drain the last drops from our glasses and the final notes of our tales fade into the night, we find ourselves at the end of our journey through the backroads and hidden corners of the American South. But like any good traveler knows, every ending is just the beginning of a new adventure.

Throughout these pages, we've mixed more than just spirits and mixers. We've blended history with mystery, fact with folklore, and the familiar with the fantastical. Each cocktail has been more than just a drink – it's been a key, unlocking stories that might otherwise have remained untold.

From the haunting whispers of Athens to the shadowy secrets of the Sayre House, from the bittersweet memories of Savannah to the unexpected connections forged in small-town diners, we've discovered that every place holds a story, waiting for someone to listen, to taste, to experience.

As you close this book, I hope you carry with you not

just recipes for libations but a thirst for the stories that surround us all. May you look at your own hometown with fresh eyes, seeing the extraordinary in the ordinary and the magic in the mundane.

Remember, dear reader, that you too are a part of this grand tapestry of tales. Your own experiences, your own cocktail creations, your own adventures – they all add to the rich, intoxicating blend that makes up our shared human experience.

So the next time you mix a drink, whether it's a sophisticated Old Fashioned or a simple Jack and Coke, take a moment to raise your glass. Toast to the stories you've read, the ones you've lived, and the ones yet to come. Toast to the unexpected detours, the chance encounters, and the moments of connection that make life a journey worth taking.

And who knows? Perhaps someday, in some far-flung corner of the world, you'll find yourself sharing a drink with a stranger, spinning yarns about the places you've been and the people you've met. In that moment, you'll know that you've become a part of the story – a postmodern gypsy in your own right, carrying the spirit of these tales forward.

Until our paths cross again, may your glass be full, your stories rich, and your journey always be interesting. Let's toast to the journey ahead and all the tales awaiting our telling, one sip at a time.